Santa's
CHRISTMAS
Storybook

Santa's CHRISTMAS Storybook

BY SANTA CLAUS

ARIEL BOOKS

Turner Publishing, Inc.

ATLANTA

Library of Congress Cataloging-in-Publication Data
Black, Sheila (Sheila Fiona)
Santa's Christmas Storybook / by Sheila Black. — 1st ed.
p.   cm.
Summary: Includes eleven stories that capture the magic of Christmas, told by Santa to the elves and all the merry people who live and work at the North Pole.
ISBN 1-57036-159-2
1. Santa Claus—Juvenile fiction.   2. Children's stories,
American.   [1. Santa Claus—Fiction.   2. Christmas—Fiction.
3. Short Stories.]   I. Title.
PZ7.B5294San 1995   95-3010
[Fic]—dc20   CIP
AC

Published by Turner Publishing, Inc.
A Subsidiary of Turner Broadcasting System, Inc.
1050 Techwood Drive, N.W.
Atlanta, Georgia 30318

Distributed by Andrews and McMeel
A Universal Press Syndicate Company
4900 Main Street
Kansas City, Missouri 64112

First Edition
10 9 8 7 6 5 4 3 2 1

Produced by Ariel Books
Art direction by Judith Stagnitto-Abbate
Book design and layout by Judith Stagnitto-Abbate
Design consulting by Michael J. Walsh
Edited by Julia Banks, Katherine Buttler, Michele Meyers
Production by Anne Murdoch

Printed in Singapore

CONTENTS

CHRISTMAS TREE SOUP

ONCE LONG AGO, a young man was wending his way home through a great pine forest. It was the day before Christmas, and he carried a knapsack full of presents on his back. He had spent all his money on gifts for his family, and he had nothing left for food or lodging. However, the young man was hardy and cheerful, so he didn't mind too much—until it started to snow.

It snowed and snowed. Great drifts of snow gathered on the tree branches and piled up around the tree trunks. The snow rose higher and higher around the young man's boots so that he had to walk ever more slowly. Soon he began to grow very hungry, for trudging through all that deep snow was hard work.

"If only I had some money," the young man said to himself, "I could stop at an inn for the night. And if only I had some bread, I could have a bite of supper." But since he had neither, there was nothing to do but keep going.

Evening was approaching; the air was twilight blue. No matter what direction the young man looked in, he could see nothing but pine trees, the kind that people use for Christmas trees. The young man smiled to think he was walking through a whole forest of Christmas trees.

"They are awfully pretty," he said to himself. "And they smell so good. If only they were good to eat, too!" The idea of eating a Christmas tree was so ridiculous that the

young man laughed out loud. As he continued to trudge through the snow, he made up a song about it:

Bubbledy, bubbledy, blubber, and bloop!
Make me a pot of Christmas tree soup!
A great big bowl of green, slimy goop!
Make me a pot of Christmas tree soup!
Oh, the only delicacy for me
Is soup made out of a Christmas tree!

He sang the song once, and it pleased him so much that he sang it again. He even picked up a large branch of pine that was lying across his path and waved it in the air. Just then a voice from not very far away called out: "Be quiet! There's folks working here, and you're making a horrible racket."

Peering into the gloom, the young man discovered that he had been walking alongside an enormous manor house. He could see that the house belonged to a wealthy lord, for it was very large, with all sorts of towers and turrets. A window on the ground floor had been thrown open, and a man wearing a tall white cook's hat was leaning out of it, shaking his fist in the young man's direction. "Well," the young man thought, "this is the first good luck I've had all day. He must be the cook of the manor. Now I'll surely be able to get some supper."

The young man took off his cap and bowed low. "Greetings, my

2

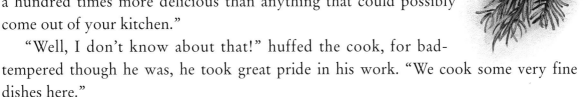

good sir," he said. "Could you please spare a poor hungry traveler a bite to eat?"

But the cook, who was a bad-tempered sort, only shook his head. "No, I could not," he snapped. "My lordship doesn't believe in giving handouts to tramps. Especially at Christmastime. He says it only encourages them."

"I don't think I would like your lordship very much," said the young man under his breath.

"What was that?" said the cook.

"Oh, nothing," said the young man. He looked down at the pine branch in his hand, and suddenly he had an idea. "I was just saying that it makes no difference whether you feed me or not. After all, I can easily make myself a nice pot of Christmas tree soup, which is a hundred times more delicious than anything that could possibly come out of your kitchen."

"Well, I don't know about that!" huffed the cook, for bad-tempered though he was, he took great pride in his work. "We cook some very fine dishes here."

"I'm sure you do," said the young man kindly. "But I must tell you, I have eaten in many grand homes as well as with the kings of England, France, and Spain. I have dined on roast peacock and grilled trout and pheasant stuffed with wild truffles—but never ever have I eaten any dish that can compare with a steaming bowl of Christmas tree soup."

The cook frowned. "Is that a fact?" he said. "How do you make this Christmas tree soup of yours?" (His lordship had often told the cook that truly great chefs were always on the lookout for new and exciting recipes.)

The young man grinned. "It's simple," he said. "It's Christmas tree soup, isn't it?" He waved the pine branch in his hand. "It's made with Christmas trees, of course."

The cook's eyes opened wide. "You must be mad," he exclaimed. "You can't make soup out of a Christmas tree!"

"Can't you?" said the young man. He leaned toward the cook and lowered his voice. "You certainly can! It's all a question of knowing the secret."

3

The cook's eyes opened wider. "The secret?"

"The secret spell," replied the young man solemnly. "Taught to me by a descendant of the great wizard Merlin. Though, of course," he added hastily, "it only works at Christmastime."

"I see. Yes. Of course," said the cook. He was quite excited by this time. He had heard about magic pots that cooked whatever you wanted if you just asked politely, and magic tablecloths that set out a meal when the right words were spoken, and many other remarkable things. Yet he had never actually seen any such miraculous happenings. But Christmas tree soup—that was bound to be something!

"Why don't you come in?" said the cook in a rush, opening the kitchen door. "You may cook your soup in here if you like."

The young man pretended to think this over. "Very well," he said. "If you're sure I won't be any bother. Just fetch me a large pot and I'll get right to work."

So the cook brought a pot which the young man filled with water and set on the fire to boil. When the water was boiling nicely, he put the pine branch in the pot. Then he waved his hands over the boiling water and chanted:

> *Bubbledy, Bubbledy, blubber, and bloop!*
> *Oh, make me a pot of Christmas tree soup!*

"Now, we'll leave it to cook a while," said the young man, "and soon you will taste the finest soup you've ever had in your life." Before long the pot was bubbling away merrily. The cook went back to his own cooking. The young man sat by the fire, happy to be in a warm kitchen and out of the cold snowy night.

Blip, blip went the water boiling in the pot. Little by little the pine needles grew soggy and goopy. The smell of pine filled the kitchen. It was a nice enough smell to be sure, but not exactly the sort of smell one expects from soup. The cook frowned and wondered if the Christmas tree soup was really cooking as it should. But the young man simply gave the pot a good stir and said, "It's coming along nicely." Then he pretended to taste a spoonful and smacked his lips. "Mmm—perfection!" he said.

The cook glanced over the young man's shoulder into the pot. The soup was murky

and green—it didn't exactly look like anything fit to eat. But the young man seemed quite delighted with it. "Mmmmm," he said, giving the pot another stir. "I think it's about ready now. This is just how the king of England likes it. Now, be a good fellow, and fetch us some bowls and prepare yourself for a feast!"

The cook hesitated a moment, for the Christmas tree soup really looked quite awful. But then he remembered that the young man had dined with the kings of England, France, and Spain. "Perhaps it's only that I haven't tasted many newfangled and rare dishes," he thought. "After all, the great chefs of the world are always experimenting." So he did as the young man asked.

With a flourish, the young man served up two bowls of thick green goop. "I'd let it cool a minute," he said, setting the steaming bowls on the table. "And a slice of bread is always nice with a bowl of Christmas tree soup."

The cook cut two slices of bread. The young man took a bite of bread. Then he took a spoonful of Christmas tree soup. "Superb! Delicious! Delectable!" he said, smacking his lips.

The cook tried a spoonful of soup. Blech! It tasted exactly like a mouthful of soggy pine needles. "Phooey!" the cook shouted. "This is horrible!" And he ran to get a glass of water.

While the cook's back was turned, the young man hastily dumped his bowl of soup back into the pot. When the cook turned around again, the young man was scraping his spoon loudly against his empty bowl, as if he were trying to scoop up every last drop.

The cook looked at the bowl, and he looked at the young man. "You've eaten it all?" he cried in astonishment. "I don't know how you can stand the stuff!"

"And I don't know how you cannot stand it," replied the young man. "Why, I haven't had such a delicious bowl of Christmas tree soup since I dined with the king of France last Christmas, and he proclaimed that soup the finest he'd ever tasted."

The cook opened his mouth and closed it again. He thought the soup was the worst he'd ever tasted. But if the king of France was so fond of it, then it must not be so bad. He tried another spoonful. "Yech!" The second spoonful was even worse than the first. "Why, it's horrible," the cook sputtered, "even on my worst days I make better soup than this!"

"You do?" The young man pretended to be utterly amazed. "I don't believe it. I can't believe it. You must be a very remarkable cook if you can make better soup than this."

"Well, I . . ." said the cook, flattered.

"Indeed, the kings of England, France, and Spain would be very interested to hear about this," continued the young man, "for each of them has told me that Christmas tree soup is his very favorite dish. If you can make a soup better than this, why, I'm sure they'll want the recipe. How do you do it? What is your secret?"

"It's simple really," said the old cook, trying to be modest about his great skill. "I just take some onions, and some carrots, oh, and a plump chicken or two, and I—"

"Please slow down," said the young man. "I want to make sure I understand."

7

The cook tried to speak more slowly, but the young man still said he couldn't quite follow the recipe. "Perhaps you had better show me how you make your soup," he suggested, "for I wouldn't want to leave out anything when I tell the royal chefs for the kings of England, France, and Spain how it is made."

At that the cook decided he needed to show the young man exactly how to make his soup. So he put carrots, onions, a whole turkey (instead of two plump chickens), potatoes, and mushrooms all together in a big pot of water. Then he added salt, pepper, and other special seasonings and set it on the flame to boil.

The soup took a long time to cook, much longer than the Christmas tree soup. But the young man didn't mind. He was glad to be safely indoors and out of the cold. Still, he was getting hungrier every minute, so he was very glad when the cook finally announced that his soup was ready.

With a flourish, the old cook ladled out a bowlful and gave it to the young man. "Now, taste that," he said, "and tell me if it isn't better than your Christmas tree soup."

As the cook looked on eagerly, the young man took one spoonful, then another, and then he spooned up the entire bowl lickety-split.

"Hmm," he said. "Not bad. But I wonder what the king of England would say. He's very particular, you know. Perhaps I better try another bowl before I decide."

So the cook served the young man another bowl, which he promptly gobbled down almost as quickly as the first. "This soup is tasty," he said. "But I wonder what the king of France would think. He's very fond of Christmas tree soup. Perhaps I better try another bowl, just to be certain."

So the cook served the young man a third bowl.

He gobbled that up, too, though not quite as quickly as the first two. "Well," he said when he was done. "I take my hat off to you. Your Christmas tree soup is even better than mine. The kings of England, France, and Spain will be delighted. Sir, you are indeed a champion cook of Christmas tree soup."

"But," the cook frowned, "there are no Christmas trees in my soup!"

The young man grinned and pulled on his cloak. "No there, aren't," he agreed cheerfully. "But it's still Christmas tree soup to me, for it was like a gift under a Christmas tree. And one I was much in need of," he added, quickly stepping out the door before the cook, who realized he had been fooled, could grab hold of him. Wishing the cook a "Merry Christmas," the young man sped on his way—whistling happily all the while:

Bubbledy, bubbledy, blubber, and bloop!
Make me a pot of Christmas tree soup!
A great big bowl of green, slimy goop!
Make me a pot of Christmas tree soup!
Oh, the only delicacy for me
Is soup made out of a Christmas tree!

SNOWBALL, THE NAUGHTY CHRISTMAS KITTEN

*I*T WAS SNOWING OUTSIDE, but inside the farmhouse kitchen it was warm and cozy. A fire was burning in the hearth, and there was a smell of currants and nutmeg, for it was two days before Christmas and the plum puddings had just been made. A large gray tabby cat named Mrs. Tiddlywinks sat curled up in front of the fire. She narrowed her eyes thoughtfully as she watched three kittens—one black, one calico, and one that was white as a snowball—playing beneath the big farmhouse table.

"They are sweet little creatures, aren't they, Shep?" she asked the old hound dog stretched out beside her.

Now, some people who don't know any better insist that cats and dogs can't possibly get along. But the gray tabby and the old hound were the best of friends. This was why old Shep knew exactly what Mrs. Tiddlywinks was thinking, even though she didn't say another word.

"They certainly are," he said heartily. "And don't worry, Mrs. T. I'm sure you'll have

11

no trouble finding them good homes." He lowered his voice a notch. "When does she want them gone?"

She was the farmhouse cook, and ever since the farmer's wife (who had been a great friend to Mrs. Tiddlywinks) had died, Cook had ruled the household with an iron hand.

"She says Christmas at the latest," sighed Mrs. Tiddlywinks. "But I do so want them to be close by. Sooty," that was the name of the black kitten, "is turning into an excellent mouser, just like me, and Patch," that was the calico one, "is so sweet-tempered, I'm sure anyone would be glad to have them. But I do worry about Snowball."

Snowball was the white kitten. Shep secretly thought Mrs. Tiddlywinks was right to worry about him, for he was very mischievous. However, the old hound knew better than to say such a thing to a mother. "Now, now, Mrs. T.," he said. "Snowball will turn out all right, you'll see."

Just then there was a tremendous crash. The white kitten had been chasing his brother and sister across the dish cabinet when he knocked over the giant china platter Cook always used for the Sunday roast. The platter now lay in pieces on the floor.

"Oh, Snowball!" cried Mrs. Tiddlywinks. "How could you?"

The small white ball of fluff looked up at her sideways. "Sorry, Ma," he said, peering up at her with his bright blue eyes. "I didn't mean to. Honest. It was an accident!"

"I'm sure it was," said Mrs. Tiddlywinks, "but I'm afraid Cook won't—" but at that moment the door burst open, and there stood Cook herself.

When she saw the broken platter, Cook's face turned scarlet with rage. "That's the last straw!" she roared. "I've tried to be patient with you, Snowball, but now you've

gone too far! You're a wicked, bad kitten!" Cook turned to Mrs. Tiddlywinks. "I said he could stay here until you found him a home," she said, "but you better have him out of here by Christmas or I'll . . . drown him!"

Drown him! To the animals listening these were the most dreadful words ever spoken in the old farmhouse. Mrs. Tiddlywinks's beautiful green eyes turned gray with shock.

"Drown him!" Mrs. Tiddlywinks repeated. "I never thought I'd hear such a thing. Especially not here in my own home. I was born on this farm, and I was the farmer's wife's favorite. If she were alive she would never stand for this. I do wonder, Shep, if I should leave this house forever, and take my three kittens with me."

"Yes, Mama, let's," meowed Sooty and Patch. "Don't you agree, Snowball?"

Snowball didn't reply at once. Instead he gazed around the warm farmhouse kitchen. "What a pleasant place this is," he thought. "And Mama has lived here all her life. It isn't fair that she should have to leave here because I'm so naughty."

"No," Snowball said aloud. "I don't. At least, I don't think you should leave, Mama." The kitten did a somersault and landed all in a heap at his mother's paws. "You needn't worry about me, either," he went on. "I won't have any trouble finding a home. Lots of people would be delighted to have a clever kitten like me."

"Oh, they would, would they?" said Mrs. Tiddlywinks, smiling in spite of herself.

"Yes, they would," Snowball declared. "So you just stay here, Mama, and I'll go off into the world." The white kitten started for the back door.

"Oh, no, you don't, you little scamp," growled Shep, pulling Snowball back by the scruff of his neck. "You've caused enough worry for one day. Besides, I have a much better idea." The hound turned to Mrs. Tiddlywinks. "Why don't we take all three kittens to the miller's house tomorrow morning?" he suggested.

"He's an old friend of mine, and he's always on the lookout for good mousers. His wife is fond of cats, too. I'm sure they'll be glad to give your kittens a good home, Mrs. T. That way you won't have to worry about Snowball still being here at Christmas."

Mrs. Tiddlywinks's eyes lit up with relief. "Oh, Shep, thank you. That would be wonderful!"

"Then we shall be the miller's kittens?" said Sooty. "Hooray!"

"Hip-hip-hooray!" said Patch.

Snowball said, "hooray," too, but inside he was thinking that he didn't want to be the miller's cat. He wanted to go off and have adventures, and find his own home.

Before dawn the next day, Mrs. Tiddlywinks cuffed the kittens awake to prepare them for their visit to the miller's house. She washed their faces and combed their tails. She told them to stand up straight and not meow too loudly, and not to do any leaping inside the mill. "Unless you see a mouse, of course." Then she and Shep led them down the road to the miller's house.

It was a cold morning and snow was falling thickly. At first the kittens chased the fat snowflakes, but soon their paws and noses were tingling with the cold. Sooty and Patch began to complain, but not Snowflake. Since he was named for the snow, he felt the least he could do was put up with it. Nevertheless, he was glad when they finally reached the miller's home.

The miller and his wife lived on the first floor of the mill. Their house was clean and neat, and smelled of flour.

"What fine kittens," said the miller when old Shep introduced them. "Are you sure they'll make good mousers?" Shep barked and nodded. "Very well," said the miller. "We'll give them a try." He led the three kittens upstairs into the mill while Mrs. Tiddlywinks and the miller's wife looked on from the stairway.

Sooty soon found a mouse to chase. Because she liked chasing mice better than anything and practiced often, she soon caught him in her little paws. "Well done," said the miller. Patch was not such a good mouser. But he rubbed against the legs of the miller's wife and purred sweetly at her. "How adorable!" she said.

Nobody paid any attention to Snowball, which was fine with him. He was busy having fun. First, he chased his own shadow. Next, he tried to catch a drifting speck of dust between his paws. Then he looked up at the big brown sacks stacked against the mill wall. He had never seen such large sacks before, and he wondered what was inside them.

"If I poke a hole in one with my paw, perhaps I could find out," the kitten thought. He knew this was a naughty thing to do, but he couldn't help himself. He leaped up onto the nearest sack and clawed at it until he'd torn a large hole. Sssss. . . . Out streamed an avalanche of white flour, all over the floor and all over Snowball, who ran and spread it all over the miller's tidy house.

"Oh, Snowball!" cried Mrs. Tiddlywinks.

"Oh, no!" groaned Shep.

"The black kitten and the calico one are welcome to stay," said the miller, "but you better take the white one with you. He's nothing but trouble!"

The journey back from the miller's house was not nearly so pleasant for Snowball as the trip to the miller's house had been. His mother and Shep were furious with him. "How could you?" Mrs. Tiddlywinks scolded.

"You embarrassed me," huffed Shep.

"Whatever will we do with you now?" cried Mrs. Tiddlywinks. "It's only one day to Christmas."

"I dare say we'll just have to hide him somewhere," replied Shep darkly, "or Cook really may drown him." At that Mrs. Tiddlywinks began to cry.

Snowball hung his head. "I deserve to be scolded," he sniffed to himself, "especially by Mama, for I have done nothing but make trouble for her." And he decided that instead of going back to the farm and to Cook, who wanted to drown him, he would run away and find a home of his own.

The snow was falling very heavily by this time, so it was not hard for the small white kitten to slip away. Mrs. Tiddlywinks and Old Shep were dreadfully upset when they discovered him missing. But by then Snowball was quite a long way down the road. Indeed, he had already passed the miller's house and was heading toward town.

Snowball went along at a fast pace, for a kitten. But it really was hard going, trudging through all that deep snow. Before long, Snowball was so cold and tired he didn't see how he could possibly go any farther.

Just then, he spotted a long low building with lamps glowing softly inside. This building was the local creamery where the milkmaids made fresh butter and cheese every day. Snowball poked his nose inside.

"Look," cried one of the milkmaids. "It's a little white kitten." The other milkmaids came running. "How adorable," they said. "Let's bring him in and put him by the fire." They made a great fuss over Snowball and even brought him a whole dish of cream.

"Well! I can see that this place will make me a fine home," the kitten purred, feeling very pleased with himself.

After a while, the milkmaids went back to work, and Snowball was left by himself. At first, he sat quietly. But then some big milk jugs caught his eye. He wondered how heavy they were, and whether he could tip one over by jumping on it. Unfortunately, he could and he did! Fresh creamy milk spilled out all over the floor. The head milkmaid shook her head in disgust. "I should have known," she said. "Putting a cat around cream is like putting a fox among chickens!" And she carried Snowball to the door and tossed him outside.

Feeling very forlorn, Snowball started down the road again. Before he had gone very far, a carriage pulled to a halt right beside him. "Oh, look, a kitten," said an old woman. "Pick him up and give him to me." The coachman scooped up Snowball, and the next thing the kitten knew, he was inside the warm carriage. An old lady dressed in fine black lace was holding him on her knee.

"What do you think, Graykins? Isn't he a sweet little thing?" the old lady asked a large gray Persian cat, who was sitting beside her on the seat. But the Persian only turned up his nose.

"He doesn't like me much," Snowball thought. "But the old lady does, and I suppose Graykins will, too, in

16

time." But at that moment the gray Persian turned his pale blue eyes on Snowball and hissed very softly, "You may ride with us to town if you like, white kitten. But don't get any ideas. The old lady is my owner. I won't stand for any intruders. If you try to stay with us, I'll scratch your eyes out. Do you understand?"

"Y-y-es," replied Snowball, and he kept very still until the carriage pulled into town. Then he slipped away.

It had grown dark by then, and the town seemed very big and empty. The only thing cheerful about it was that all the buildings were hung with bright lights. These were Christmas lights, for it was now Christmas Eve. But Snowball didn't remember what day it was. All he knew was that he was lost and hungry, and needed a good home.

Up and down the streets Snowball went. He peered up at all the buildings, trying to muster the courage to enter one. At last, he saw many people bustling in and out of a store. Snowball quickly ducked in the doorway and was surrounded by the wonderful, warm, sweet smells of a bakery. He tiptoed among all the busy feet, looking for a quiet corner in which to rest.

Suddenly, one of the baker's assistants shouted, "Look! A giant white mouse." Snowball was so wet and bedraggled he didn't even look like a cat. "Don't be silly," said the baker. "It's only a stray kitten." He reached down and tweaked Snowball's tail. In a panic, the kitten leaped up onto the counter, knocking over a stack of plum puddings. Everyone in the bakery began shouting and chasing poor Snowball every which way.

"I definitely won't find a home here!" the kitten thought, and when no one was looking he quickly climbed into a large white box. The box contained a freshly made Bouche de Noël, a special Christmas cake made of chocolate, and iced and decorated to look like a log in the

17

forest. The Bouche de Noël was quite large, but there was just enough room for Snowball to curl up in a corner of the box. And there he stayed without moving even a whisker.

Eventually the hunt for the kitten ended and things quieted down. Yet just as Snowball was thinking it might be safe to come out again, someone lifted up the box, and Snowball felt himself being carried quickly along. Where was he going now? The kitten didn't even dare think about it. He just curled up in a tight ball and closed his little blue eyes just as tightly. He thought of Old Shep and Sooty and Patch, and most of all, of his mother, Mrs. Tiddly-winks. "If I'd only known what a big place the world is, and how scary," Snowball sighed. "I never would have been such a naughty kitten. Oh, Mama, will I ever see you again?"

The box swayed from side to side and at times it bounced a little. After what seemed like a long time to Snowball, the box was set down in a quiet place. Snowball sat up and poked at the lid of the box, but it was tied shut. He was stuck! He rubbed his eyes with his paws, and then, because he was very hungry, he started to eat some of the cake.

Now, unlike most people (especially young people), cats are not very fond of sugar icing, chocolate, or indeed, any kind of sweet. But Snowball was so hungry that he not only ate the chocolate bark icing off the Christmas log, but even the frosted mushrooms and most of the chocolate sponge cake. Then, feeling not only sad but also rather sick, he drifted off to sleep.

Snowball awoke when the box was hoisted high into the air. "Here's the box from the bakery with the Christmas log in it," said a man's voice. "Who wants to open it?"

"I do, Uncle," a little girl's voice replied.

"All right, go on and cut the ribbon." Snowball was set down with a bump, and the box was opened. The kitten found himself staring up at a little girl with blonde hair, a stubborn mouth, and a pair of mischievous blue eyes.

"Oh, Uncle! What a fine trick. You've gotten me a Christmas kitten!"

"No, I didn't get you a kitten," said her uncle. "What in the world are you talking about, Amanda? There's a Christmas cake in that box. A real Bouche de Noël."

"Well, maybe there was," replied Amanda, with a grin. "It's mostly crumbs now. But there is a kitten in this box. And even if you didn't mean to get him for me, he's mine now. I can tell that we're going to be great friends."

"I think she's right, Charles," said Amanda's mother. Snowball knew it was her mother because the lady sounded so much like his own mother, Mrs. Tiddlywinks. "This kitten looks as if he's almost as much of a troublemaker as Amanda is. I'll bet they'll get along splendidly."

"I know we will," Amanda said. She hugged Snowball tightly. For once Snowball didn't squirm or do anything the least bit naughty, for he knew that he had truly found a home.

"I shall call him Snowball," Amanda declared, guessing his name by the queer magic by which pets and their proper owners always recognize each other. "And he shall always be my Christmas kitten."

And so Snowball was, even when he was no longer a kitten and no longer naughty, but a very large, grand white cat. Indeed, Snowball grew so grand that when Amanda took him in her carriage the following Christmas to visit the farmhouse where he'd been born, Old Shep didn't even recognize him. But Mrs. Tiddlywinks did. "It's Snowball," she cried happily. "My own little Snowball. Why, I'd know those mischievous blue eyes anywhere."

19

ICHOD,
THE ICE TROLL

*E*VERYONE KNOWS THAT Santa Claus lives at the North Pole. And just about everyone has heard about Santa's secret toy workshop, his elves, and his magic sleigh and reindeer. But what most people don't know is that the North Pole is also home to many other creatures.

All sorts of marvelous creatures live in that remote snowy land—polar bears, puffins, and ice wolves, to name a few. Yet there are also other stranger beings—gnomes, fairies, and sprites—that have been there even longer than Santa Claus himself.

Most are delightful creatures. There are ice sprites, whose job it is to deliver presents to the polar residents, and frost fairies, who paint glistening pictures on windows in the wintertime. But the North Pole is also home to several less pleasant characters. And at the time our story begins, the nastiest of these was Ichod, the ice troll.

No one knew how Ichod first came to the North Pole, but he had lived in an ice cave deep under the snow for as long as anyone could remember. Some said he had been left behind by mistake a long, long time ago as his family traveled to the ice trolls' annual gathering in the icy fjords of Norway. But whatever the true story was, Ichod was the only ice troll at the North Pole, and he had no friends or relations. Perhaps it was living

alone in the chilly darkness that had made Ichod what he was, for he seemed to have a cube of ice where his heart should have been.

Ichod hated almost everything and everyone. And what he didn't hate left him indifferent. He passed his days stamping about, sneering and scowling. Everywhere he went, Ichod carried a big slingshot, which he called his toy. He amused himself by loading this slingshot with balls of ice and firing them at every living thing that crossed his path.

The snow geese and owls soared high into the air whenever they saw Ichod coming. The walruses and seals swam away as fast as they could when they spotted the tip of Ichod's long nose. Even the polar bears, who are pretty fierce themselves, kept well out of Ichod's way.

This made Ichod happy, for he hated these wild creatures more than anything—except Santa Claus. Ichod despised Santa Claus. He despised Mrs. Claus and Santa's elves and Santa's reindeer, too. Indeed, the mere mention of anything that had to do with Santa Claus made him stamp his feet and jump up and down in fury. And the word *Christmas* made Ichod so angry he tore at his hair and howled out loud, for he hated Christmas most of all.

This was because Christmas was the favorite time of the year of everyone else in the North Pole. Each year at Christmastime the air became full of the sound of Christmas carols. Elves, fairies, sprites, and gnomes bustled about making one another Christmas presents and preparing for their Christmas celebrations. Even the animals and birds took part in holiday preparations, decorating their caves, burrows, and nests with branches of holly and strings of colored lights. Meanwhile, year after year, Ichod watched and brooded from his dark, cold cave, and his heart grew harder and colder.

"Why don't they just shut up," the troll

snarled to himself one year. "Don't they know that I hate noise? What in the world are they singing about, anyway?"

And Ichod sat in his shivery dark cave and thought about how much he hated every last thing about Christmas.

He hated smelling the good food everyone else was busy cooking in honor of the holiday. "For they won't give me any," Ichod growled. "Not that I'd want it anyway," he added, chewing on a stale, cold crust of bread.

He hated hearing the other residents of the North Pole talk about the presents they wanted and the presents they were giving. "Why should they all get presents," Ichod groused, "when no one gives presents to me? Not that I'd want them anyway," he added, pulling at the rope on his slingshot to make it twang.

"If only I could put a stop to this whole Christmas business!" Ichod declared. "I would bury Christmas so deep in the cold and dark that no one would ever find it again." A smile slowly spread over Ichod's sour face. "Yes," he hissed, "somehow I must put an end to Christmas."

Ichod sat and thought. It would not be easy to put a stop to Christmas. He had heard that people all over the world loved Christmas. "If only I could get rid of all those stupid, sticky-icky Christmas lovers," Ichod snapped. But how? There were so many of them, and there was only one Ichod.

"Perhaps I could hypnotize them!" the troll thought, "or cast a spell on them to make them hate Christmas and Santa Claus as much as I do!" But then Ichod shook his head. He had tried to hypnotize people before; it had never worked. And the only spell he knew was for giving people frostbite. The spell worked every time he used it, for dark and cold were what Ichod knew and liked best. It was a nasty little spell, but not nearly nasty enough to stop Christmas.

"Perhaps I could kidnap Santa Claus," Ichod thought. But he knew that wouldn't work either. Everyone in almost the whole world knew Santa Claus! If he kidnapped

him, they all would be out looking for him in no time. "And chances are they would find him," Ichod muttered.

Suddenly, a ghastly smile spread over Ichod's face. "Of course," the troll chortled, for he had just had a brilliant idea. "What is it that makes everyone love Christmas? Presents! People love Christmas, and they love Santa Claus because he brings them toys. If I make sure there are no more toys, soon everyone will hate Santa and Christmas just as I do. But how can I do that?" he wondered.

And then he smiled again.

You see, in all the years Ichod had been prowling around the North Pole, he had learned a great deal about Santa and his elves. Ichod knew which elves worked in Santa's mailroom, which elves wrapped presents, and which elves took care of the reindeer. Most important, Ichod knew that Santa's chief toymaker and toy designer was an elf named Hamlin.

Hamlin had been with Santa longer than anyone except Mrs. Claus. Santa had often been heard to say he didn't know how he would do his job without trusty Hamlin. "That's it!" crowed Ichod. "I'll kidnap Hamlin, and I won't give him back until Santa Claus promises to stop Christmas forever." The troll threw back his head and laughed so long and loud that a big crack formed in the ceiling of his cave.

That very night Ichod put his plan into operation. Silent as a shadow, he crept to Santa's workshop. He had his slingshot in one hand and a heavy cloth sack in the other. Peering through the workshop window, he watched as the elves put their tools away and left for the night. As usual, Hamlin, the master toymaker elf, stayed later than the others. Ichod waited until Hamlin turned out the workshop light and started toward the door.

Ichod grinned.

"Goodbye, Christmas," he hissed. He put a big ball of hard ice in his slingshot and fired. Bam! It hit Hamlin in the

24

back of the head. The elf fell down, stunned. With a horrible chuckle, Ichod stuffed Hamlin into his sack. The troll then pinned this note to Santa's workshop door: "S. Claus. BE WARNED. If you ever want to see your employee HAMLIN ELF again, you must STOP CHRISTMAS FOREVER! Right Now! Or Else!"

"Ha, ha, ha. Ho, ho, ho," said Ichod. He slung the sack over his shoulder, and dragged Hamlin back to his cold, dark cave.

When Ichod's note was discovered, the whole North Pole was in an uproar. No one could guess who had kidnapped Hamlin or where he had been taken. Worse still, Christmas was only a day and a half away! Not only did all the Christmas toys still need their finishing touches, but neither Santa Claus nor the other elves could imagine Christmas without Hamlin elf. Santa had to save his old friend, but how could he possibly agree to stop Christmas forever? All the residents of the North Pole were upset—except Ichod, of course.

Whistling to himself, the troll chained Hamlin to a huge block of ice. "Hah!" Ichod gloated gleefully. "I knew I could stop Christmas if I tried." He snapped his fingers under Hamlin's nose and danced around his cave. "Thanks to my brilliant plan, there's no more you, and no more toys. And soon there will be no more Santa Claus, and no more Christmas, either!"

Ichod's eyes glittered like two round ice cubes. "Why, the very idea almost warms my cold, cold heart. No more runny-nosed little kids tearing open their presents on Christmas morning. No more Christmas trees or candy canes or ho-ho-hos or sleighs or reindeer! No more Christmas! Hooray!"

Hamlin elf just looked at him. "That's what you think," he said calmly.

"What do you mean, that's what I think?" Ichod scoffed. "You mean to say your pal, Santa Claus, won't even try to rescue you? Some hero! Besides," Ichod went on, "even if Mr. S. Claus doesn't agree to my demands, without you there won't be any toys, and without toys there won't be any Christmas. So either way I win."

"That's what you think," Hamlin elf said again.

This time Ichod shoved his long nose right in Hamlin's face and glared at him. "Shut up," he bellowed, "or I'll make you shut up!" The troll stepped back and crossed his arms. "I know what you're up to," he sniffed. "You're trying to make me nervous. Well, it won't work. I said I was going to stop Christmas and I have.

"So go on and make yourself at home, Mr. Elf. I'm going out and leaving you here. And if Santa doesn't agree to my demands soon, here is where you'll stay, forever. The whole world will soon forget about your precious Christmas then. Who's going to love Christmas without any toys?"

Ichod roared with laughter, making the crack in his ceiling widen another six inches, then stamped out into the North Pole night, his slingshot in hand.

All that long dark Christmas Eve, the miserable troll skulked about, watching and listening. Everywhere he went, everyone was worried about Hamlin elf and worried about what Santa would do. Would Santa go out and risk never seeing Hamlin again? Or would he stay home and disappoint children all over the world? Either way Christmas would surely be ruined.

Ichod was overjoyed. "I am Ichod, Stopper of Christmas this year and every year!" the troll exulted as the moon rose and the stars crept out. He tiptoed over to Santa's workshop and peeked in the windows. Everything was dark and quiet. There was no sign of Santa Claus or his elves or his sleigh or his reindeer.

"Christmas is finished," Ichod cried. "I've won!" He loaded his slingshot with ice balls and fired them into the air in celebration. It was almost Christmas morning. Ichod hastily started home, for he didn't want to be out when the sun rose.

But as Ichod neared his cave, he heard a most peculiar sound. "Pom, pom, pom," it went, like tiny drums beating. And then: "ta-da, ta-da, ta-da," like the blaring of tiny brass trumpets.

"What's all this racket?" stormed Ichod, and he sped up his pace. A few steps from

his front door, the troll stopped and sniffed. Not only was there a strange noise, but there was a funny smell as well. It was a smell Ichod remembered . . . a smell like raisins, nuts, and dough all cooking together. A smell like . . . "Christmas!" Ichod roared. He raced to the entrance of his cave, noticing that there was a light coming from under the door. It was a light that changed from red to green and back again . . . a light like Christmas!

Ichod threw open the door. "What's going on here?" he shrieked in a dreadful rage.

His mouth fell open. His dark, cold cave was no longer dark or cold. A fire was burning in the center of it—a fire made of newspapers and bits of wood Ichod had filched from his neighbors over the years. The light the fire gave off was red and green. The colors of Christmas! But that was not all. . . .

Over the fire hung Ichod's own rusty copper pot, in which he sometimes cooked some gruel when he had a cold. The pot was no longer rusty, but polished and bright. It was not gruel that was cooking in it either, but Christmas pudding.

As if this were not bad enough, on the floor in front of the fire was a bright object, the like of which Ichod had never seen before. The object was spinning around, and as it

spun, it made the sounds Ichod had heard on his way home. "Pom, pom, pom! Ta-da, ta-da, ta-da!" It was a melody—the melody of a song Ichod faintly remembered. "We wish you a merry Christmas, we wish you a merry Christmas . . ."

Ichod frowned. "What is this thing?" he howled.

Hamlin, who had used a little elf magic to slip his chains when the troll left the cave, smiled at him. "It's a toy," he replied. "A toy carousel. I made it for you, for Christmas."

"For Christmas?" the troll raged. "How dare you! I don't want any toys. I don't want any presents. I hate Christmas!"

Ichod picked up the toy carousel, intending to throw it in the fire, but he stopped when he noticed what a clever little gadget it was. The carousel was made entirely out of polished tin. In fact, it was made out of the old tin cans Ichod kept piled up in the darkest, dingiest corner of his cave. They had been cut and polished to make a perfect little carousel, only instead of horses, the carousel had tiny reindeer and polar bears riding around and around on it. "Pom, pom, pom!" the carousel went as it spun around. "Ta-da, ta-da, ta-da! We wish you a merry Christmas . . ."

Suddenly, Ichod noticed that one of the tiny reindeer had someone riding on its back. That someone looked familiar. Ichod stared. Why, it was a tiny model of him, and he was smiling.

"But that's me!" Ichod cried, dumbfounded.

"Of course it's you," said Hamlin. "It's your carousel, isn't it? It's only right that you ride on your own carousel."

"I suppose you have a point," said Ichod. He felt very surprised and sort of funny. He took a step toward the brightly burning fire Hamlin had made. He was going to kick

it and scatter the glowing embers, but he felt the cheering warmth and saw the pudding bubbling in the pot. It was almost ready and smelled delicious. He stopped. A curious thing was happening—there was a crack and a small, hissing sigh, like an ice cube thawing, and a slow smile spread over Ichod's face. He felt a funny warm spark deep in his chest, for his ice heart was melting and melting.

"No one ever gave me a present of my very own before," Ichod, the ice troll, said.

"I know," said Hamlin. "Merry Christmas."

"M-m-erry Christmas," stammered Ichod. Somehow Christmas didn't seem such a very bad thing after all. On the contrary, it seemed to Ichod that Christmas was something bright and wonderful, like the smile on Hamlin's friendly face as he stirred the pudding over the fire. He could understand now why the elves, sprites, and fairies bustled about preparing gifts and surprises for each other. Suddenly Ichod knew what he had to do. He took Hamlin back to Santa's workshop where Santa and the other elves were waiting anxiously. There wasn't much time, but with Ichod's help, Santa and the elves managed to load all the presents (which the other elves had finished without Hamlin's help, after all) onto the sleigh. So off Santa went—in the nick of time—to bring Christmas to everyone around the world.

And every year since, Ichod has helped Santa and his elves load the sleigh on Christmas Eve. And the residents of the North Pole now call him "Friend Ichod," or "Ichod, the Christmas Troll."

THE PERFECT
CHRISTMAS PRESENT

*H*AVE YOU DECIDED on a present yet?"
Meg asked her little brother. Charles Osborne pulled off his mittens and shoved them in his pocket. "No," he said. "There's lots of stuff here, but nothing perfect." He pronounced the word with extra-special care. Charles Osborne had just turned six, and the word "perfect" had only recently been added to his vocabulary.

"Oh, Charles Osborne, there's no such thing as the perfect present. Just choose something. Mom will like whatever you get her." Charles Osborne's chin jutted out. "No," he said. "It has to be *perfect*."

Meg groaned. "All right," she said, "we'll go look in the ladies gloves-and-scarves department one more time."

Charles followed his sister across the main floor of Saxon's Department Store. Giant paper cut-outs of Santa Claus and his reindeer hung from the ceiling. It was Christmas Eve, "The last shopping day before Christmas," Meg reminded him.

Meg held up a pair of blue woolen gloves. "What about these?" she said. Charles shook his head. "Too *boring*." That was another word he had just learned. "Then how

31

about one of those plaid scarves?" Meg suggested. "They're on sale." Her voice sounded impatient. "Uh-uh." Charles said.

He turned away from the scarves and gloves and glanced over at the jewelry department. There were all kinds of shiny earrings, necklaces, and bracelets there, but most of them probably cost too much money. Charles Osborne sighed. Then he spotted it: the *perfect* present.

It was a hat, a wonderful hat. It was hanging from a hook against the wall of the hat department, a long knitted hat made of bright red wool. It looked almost like a Santa Claus hat, but it was even longer than that. It was so long that if Charles Osborne put it on it would reach all the way to the floor.

"There it is!" Charles shouted.

"What?"

"The perfect present! That hat!"

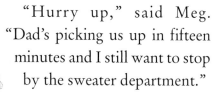

"Okay," Meg grumbled. "You don't have to shout." But she didn't really sound mad. She and Charles marched over to the hat department, and Meg went up to the lady behind the counter. "Can we see that hat please?" she asked. "How much does it cost?"

The lady behind the counter smiled. "Oh, our snow elf hat," she said. "Cute, isn't it? It's five dollars and fifty cents."

Charles Osborne frowned. "But I only have five dollars," he whispered to his sister.

"Don't worry," Meg told him. "I'll pay for the rest."

A moment later, the wonderful hat was in a bag, and the bag was in Charles Osborne's hand. He felt so happy he thought he would burst. He kept thinking about how surprised his mother would be when she saw the beautiful red hat.

"Hurry up," said Meg. "Dad's picking us up in fifteen minutes and I still want to stop by the sweater department."

"Okay." Charles Osborne followed his big sister across the store. There were more people here now, so many that Charles Osborne felt a little dizzy looking around at them all. He opened his mouth and yawned. He was starting to feel hot and sleepy.

"Hurry up," said Meg. "We don't have much time."

Charles followed her past ladies coats and dresses and on to the sweaters. He stood quietly by while Meg tried on a blue turtleneck, and then a big yellow pullover. Sweaters were boring, boring, boring, Charles Osborne thought to himself.

"Oh, no!" said Meg. "We were supposed to meet Dad five minutes ago!" She took Charles Osborne's hand and yanked him toward the door. Meg's legs were longer than his, so when she walked quickly, it was hard for him to keep up.

"Meg! Charles! Over here." Their father was waving at them.

It was then that Charles Osborne realized that his hands were empty. The bag holding the precious red hat, his perfect present, was gone!

"Where did you leave it?" his father asked him. Charles Osborne thought and thought, but he couldn't remember. "I don't know. I had it one minute, and then it was gone!" Meg shook her head. "Oh, Charles," she said.

Charles swallowed. He was six years old now and too big to cry about every little thing. But this wasn't a little thing.

He followed his father and Meg to all the places they had been. They asked at the jewelry counter and in the sweater department if anyone had seen a bag with a red hat in it, but no one had. They

33

even went back to the lady at the hat counter, and asked if anyone had turned in the bag with the wonderful red hat in it, but no one had.

"Now I don't have anything to give Mom for Christmas," declared Charles Osborne.

"Don't worry," said his father. "Your mother will understand. Anyway, I bought her two presents. You can give her one of them if you like."

"That's okay," Charles said.

"Maybe you could make her something," Meg suggested.

"Like what?" he asked. But no one answered.

"What's the matter, Charles Osborne?" his mother asked him that night at dinner. "It's Christmas Eve, and you're not even smiling."

"Nothing," Charles said. He looked at his father and Meg. He had made them promise not to tell his mother what had happened. "If you tell Mom I lost her perfect present, I will never talk to you again," he had told them.

After dinner Charles Osborne went straight up to his room and flopped down on his bed.

Meg knocked on his door. "Don't you want to come help decorate the tree?" she said.

"No," said Charles Osborne.

His mother knocked on his door. "Don't you want to come help make Christmas cookies for Santa?" she said.

"No," said Charles Osborne.

His father knocked on the door. "Hey, Charles, come on downstairs," he said. "No one is having any fun without you."

"Just leave me alone," said Charles Osborne.

He put his pillow over his head. All he

could think about was the wonderful red hat. How could he have found the perfect Christmas present and then lost it? Now not only did he not have the perfect present for his mother, he didn't have *any* present for her. He had to do something—fast!—but what?

"Make something." Meg had said. But what could he make?

Charles Osborne looked around his room. In the corner he spotted the big pad of paper and watercolor paints his mother had given him for his birthday. Suddenly, Charles Osborne had an idea.

He fetched a glass of water from the bathroom. He tore a sheet of paper from the pad and opened the new box of paints. He dipped his brush in the water and started to paint.

Charles painted Saxon's Department Store just as it had been when he and Meg had gone shopping for the perfect present. He painted the cut-out Santa Clauses and reindeer, and all the people shopping for Christmas presents. He even painted Meg trying on the big yellow pullover. And in the middle, he painted himself wearing the wonderful red hat. At the bottom of the picture, he wrote, THE PERFECT PRESENT WICH I LOST. SORRY MOM. MERRY CHRISTMAS. LOVE C. O.

Then he put down his brush.

His picture wasn't perfect. Charles Osborne had accidentally smudged Meg's hair with his elbow. And when he painted himself, the brush was too wet, so his eyes ran into his mouth. But in the picture the red hat looked every bit as wonderful as he remembered it.

Charles yawned. "I'll lie down here on the bed just for a minute," he thought sleepily. "Then I'll wash my face, brush my teeth, and put on my pajamas." The next thing he knew someone was shaking him awake. It was Meg.

"Wake up, Charles Osborne!" she said. "It's Christmas morning. Come see what Santa Claus brought you!"

Charles opened his eyes and looked around. Someone had put on his pajamas and tucked him in. But the picture he'd painted for his mother was right where he'd left it. Charles Osborne smiled.

"Coming," he said. He stood up and picked up his picture and followed Meg downstairs. His father and mother were already there, and under the tree was a huge pile of presents.

"Good morning, Charles Osborne," his mother said. "What's that you've got there?"

Charles held the picture out to her. "It's your Christmas present," he explained. "It's not a real present but I lost your real present, so I made you this instead."

His mother took the picture and held it up. "Thank you, Charles Osborne," she said. "It's—"

But before she could finish, Meg said. "I have a surprise for you, Charles." She pulled something out from behind her back. It was the bag with the wonderful red hat in it. "Ta-da!"

"You found it! You found it!" Charles Osborne shouted.

"I didn't," Meg replied. "The lady from the hat department did. Someone turned it in right after we left. She brought it over last night. I would have told you, but you were fast asleep."

She smiled at Charles Osborne. Charles Osborne smiled back. He gave the bag to his mother. "Here," he told her. "Here's your real present. I would have wrapped it, but . . ."

"That's okay," said his mother. She lifted the red hat out of the bag and put it on. "Oh, my!"

"Do you like it?"

"I love it. It's perfect. The perfect present." Charles Osborne's mother grinned. "But I like your picture of the perfect present even better," she said. "In fact, your picture is the most wonderful, beautiful, perfect Christmas present anyone ever gave me."

"It is?" said Charles Osborne.

"Yes, it is," his mother said.

"But why?"

"Oh," said his mother, taking him on her knee and hugging him. "Just because."

Charles Osborne knew she was telling the truth because his mother never told lies. Besides, she hung his picture up over the couch where everyone could look at it. When visitors asked her about it, she told them it was the perfect start to a perfect Christmas. And it was.

A
CHRISTMAS
ANGEL

Once upon a time, there was a poor woodcutter who lived with his wife and children deep in a great forest. The woodcutter and his wife worked as hard as they could, yet the family remained poor. Their clothes were patched and darned. And while they had enough food to keep from starving, their meals were never quite big enough to fill their bellies. This upset the woodcutter, for he loved his family dearly. "If only I could earn enough money to put a chicken on the table at Christmas," he often said. He could not even imagine buying a whole turkey or a fat goose at Christmas as the wealthier people did.

Now it so happened that one Christmas the poor woodcutter at last managed to save enough money to buy a whole chicken. Full of joy, he and his wife set off to market and bought the freshest, plumpest bird they could find.

In the part of the world where the woodcutter and his family lived, the Christmas feast was held on Christmas Eve rather than Christmas Day. And as evening fell and snow drifted down outside, the woodcutter's tiny cottage became full of delicious smells.

39

There was the smell of chicken slowly roasting in its own fat, and of potatoes being mashed with milk and butter in a big pot on the top of the stove. From the oven rose the spicy-sweet scent of apples stewing, and the warm, yeasty smell of baking bread.

The woodcutter's wife smiled as the children gathered around, sniffing the air. The woodcutter's heart was glad. This year his family would have a true Christmas feast, and for once they would all have enough to eat.

At last, the woodcutter's wife declared the chicken done. She proudly lifted it from the oven and set it in the center of the table. But just as the woodcutter lifted his knife to carve the bird, there came a knock at the door.

The woodcutter's youngest daughter ran to open it. Standing there in the snow was the poorest, thinnest, hungriest-looking beggar they had ever seen. His tattered clothes flapped around him like flags, and his eyes burned in his starved face like two great lamps. "Good evening," the stranger said. "Have you anything to spare for a poor beggar?"

"We have not a penny in the house," replied the woodcutter. "But you are welcome to come in and share our Christmas feast." The woodcutter's wife sent their eldest son to fetch a plate and a chair for their guest. So the beggar sat at the table, and the woodcutter began to carve the chicken.

It was a beautiful bird—the skin was crisp and golden, and the meat was juicy and tender. The children's mouths watered. Even the woodcutter felt he could hardly wait to eat his share. But first he served their guest.

The beggar looked so hungry and was eyeing the chicken with such longing, the woodcutter decided to give him the best part. "After all, who can say when the poor man last had a decent meal?" he thought. He cut the beggar a generous slice of the breast. But no sooner had the woodcutter set the meat before his guest than it vanished into the fellow's mouth!

"W-would you like some more?" the woodcutter's wife asked.

The beggar nodded. The woodcutter cut him another slice, and another, and another, and served him three giant helpings of potatoes besides, and half the loaf of bread. Quick as a wink, the stranger gobbled up all this food. The children gazed in amazement. They knew about hunger, but they had never seen a hungrier man.

The chicken grew bonier, and the heap of potatoes grew smaller, until all that was left for the wood-cutter and his family was a sliver of chicken and a mouthful of potatoes apiece. Yet still the beggar ate and ate: five baked apples and a dish of cream the woodcutter's wife had set aside for dessert were gone in a moment.

At last, the beggar slowly pushed away his plate. "I thank you," he said. "This is the best meal I have had in a hundred years, at least. Now allow me to give you a small gift as a token of my appreciation." The stranger pulled a bat-tered burlap sack from within his cloak and handed it to the woodcutter's wife. "You will find a tablecloth inside," he told her. "Set it on your table Christmas day, for it will bring you luck."

The woodcutter's wife promised to do so, and the stranger went out the door and vanished into the snowy darkness.

"That man ate almost all our chicken!" the children exclaimed. "And who knows when we shall ever have another one?"

"So he did," said their mother. "But poor fellow—he was starving! He needed that chicken even more than we do."

"Yes," the woodcutter agreed. "I admit that I wish the poor beggar had left us a bit more of the bird. But he couldn't help being famished. Besides, it would be a sad world indeed if folks wouldn't share what they've got." Then, to make the children feel better,

he added, "In any case, we shan't go hungry tomorrow. Your uncle promised to pass by here on his way from town with fresh loaves of Christmas bread for us."

The children were much cheered. The woodcutter and his family went to bed, and their dreams that night were especially beautiful ones. But when they woke up on Christmas morning, the house was stone cold, for the fire had gone out in the night. The bread in the oven was stale, and the cat had spilled the only jug of milk. Matters soon went from bad to worse.

Outside it was snowing so heavily the woodcutter's brother barely made it to the cottage. When he did, he announced that wolves had stolen the sack with the Christmas loaves in it. It had turned into a Christmas with nothing to eat but stale bread, and nothing to drink but cold water!

The woodcutter lit a fire, and the family gathered around. They told stories and sang songs, as was their custom on Christmas. But when darkness fell and suppertime came, the children began to weep. Even the woodcutter put his chin in his hands and sighed. The woodcutter's wife did not know what to do. Then she remembered the stranger's cloth and her promise to set it on her table Christmas day.

"It is a foolish thing to set a tablecloth on an empty table," she said to herself. "Nevertheless, it is Christmas, and we must try to make merry as best we can."

She peered into the sack the beggar had given her. She was hoping that the cloth might be an especially pretty one, but it was only an ordinary white cloth—much faded and mended.

"Still," the woodcutter's wife thought, "a promise is a promise." She shook the cloth out of the sack. But what was this? The old cloth she had glimpsed was now a tablecloth of the finest linen, radiant with color. The center was ruby red, and the border was as green as forest holly, and scattered across the cloth were gleaming silver threads woven into shimmering stars. The children's eyes grew wide, and the woodcutter lifted his head from his hands and stared at the beautiful tablecloth.

The woodcutter's wife set the cloth on the table, smoothing out the creases and straightening the folds. When the cloth was properly laid out, she stepped back to admire it. As she did so, the children cried, "Look, Mother! It's a miracle!"

The woodcutter's wife blinked and saw that where the cloth had been bare a moment before, it was now piled with dishes of food. There was a golden-brown turkey, a stuffed goose, and a ham! There were roasted potatoes and green peas, bread-and-onion dressing, and freshly roasted chestnuts. Glass dishes of nuts and jams and jellies gleamed invitingly. There were plum puddings, apple and mince pies, and freshly baked ginger biscuits. It was a feast fit for royalty.

The woodcutter's wife gazed at all this plenty in fright. "But is it—can it be—real?" she whispered. "It looks real," the woodcutter replied slowly. "And it smells real!" shouted their youngest daughter. "And it tastes real!" piped their eldest son, grabbing a ginger biscuit from the end of the table. "It is real," said a voice from the doorway, a voice strange yet familiar.

The woodcutter and his wife and children turned. There in the doorway stood the beggar of the night before. But how changed he was! He was no longer half starved and

dressed in rags. Instead, he wore clothes of a dazzling brightness, and a golden light shone all around him.

"I am the Christmas angel," said the stranger. "You fed me when I was hungry, though it cost you dearly. I have come to repay your kindness. You are good, hard-working people, but your lives have not been easy. Now your luck will change. Fortune will smile on you. But no matter how comfortable you become, I beg you to take out this cloth each year at Christmastime. And never forget to care for those less fortunate than you."

Before the woodcutter or his wife could reply, the angel vanished, leaving only a single bright star outside to mark his coming. With great joy the woodcutter fetched his brother and his family, and they all sat down and feasted to their hearts' content. When they had eaten their fill, they invited their neighbors, who also ate till they could eat no more. The next morning, the woodcutter's wife carefully put the magic cloth away.

As the angel had promised, the family's luck changed. Whenever the woodcutter went out, he found sound wood to cut and managed to sell it for a good price. Soon he bought a cow for his wife, and then two hens. The cow always gave milk, and the hens always laid twice as many eggs as expected. Little by little the wood-cutter and his family became quite comfortable. But they never forgot the angel or what it felt like to be hungry. Their house was al-ways open to strangers. And every year on Christmas Day people came from all over to join in their feast. Yet no matter how many guests showed up, there was always enough for everyone to eat, with plenty left over.

A TOY'S CHRISTMAS

*I*T WAS CHRISTMAS EVE. At Barnstable's Toys, shoppers young, old, and in-between crowded the floor, "ooh"ing and "ahh"ing at all the wonderful toys and games on display. Now Barnstable's was not only the biggest toy store in the city, it was the best. Toys of every imaginable description could be found at this store: exotic Spanish flamenco dolls wearing mantillas of handmade lace; stuffed toy tigers as large as real ones, with eyes that seemed fired with life; wooden schooners with eight workable sails and a crew of toy sailors; and games and puzzles to challenge the most clever players.

From her perch on a rack along the side wall, Henny the nurse doll, one of the more ordinary toys in the store, gazed at the shoppers. "Oh, please," Henny whispered to herself. "Please let one of them pick me!" Henny wore a neat white uniform, and in her hand she carried a nurse's case. It had a red cross on the outside, and inside it had bandages, candy pills, and other useful items. She clutched her case tightly. "I'd give anything to have a real home of my own!" Henny spoke loudly enough for the other toys on the shelf to hear her, yet softly enough so no person would ever know she'd said a word.

"We all would like a home," murmured her friend, Jax the clown, beside her. "If only we could get rid of that awful sign!" Jax rolled his eyes at the sign over their heads. "Old Merchandise," it said in ugly, big, red letters. "Reduced for Quick Sale."

Henny sighed. "I know," she said. "I wish Mrs. Dithers hadn't put that sign up today of all days!" Mrs. Dithers was the manager of Barnstable's, and none of the toys liked her much. "But I daresay she's only trying to help."

"Help!" snorted Jax. "Mrs. Dithers doesn't care about us. She only wants to be rid of us. You heard what she called us. Old junk. 'If only I could get rid of this old junk,' she said. Those were her exact words! Just because we're—" his voice shook a bit, "last year's toys."

Henny didn't reply at once. Instead, she gazed longingly at the new dolls people were buying—the shiny fairy princesses and the marvelously dressed "Dolls from Far-away Lands." And she asked herself, as she had so often before, why did shoppers pick them and not her? "Is it because they are beautiful and I am not?" she wondered silently. And aloud she said, "Perhaps Mrs. Dithers is right. Perhaps we are old junk. . . ."

"Nurse Henny! Don't ever let me hear you talk that way!" said a gruff voice. "You're certainly not old junk! Why, if I was a child, I'd much rather have a useful, interesting doll like you than one of those silly fairy princess creatures!"

"Thanks, Sollie!" Henny said, smiling at the stuffed lion who sat by her other side. Sollie the lion had been there longer than any of them, so long that his beautiful golden mane had turned gray with dust. Yet he never let himself get discouraged the way the other toys on the shelf did. "But Jax is right, you know. Mrs. Dithers's sign doesn't do much for our chances."

"No," Sollie admitted, drooping a bit. "Even Mrs. Dithers should know that no one wants to buy old merchandise for a new Christmas present." Then he brightened again. "But after Christmas, when no one has much

48

money, someone is sure to snap us up. We'll all find good homes then—you'll see!"

Henny sighed again. "Yes, Sollie, but . . ." She gazed up at the tinsel stars and snowflakes hanging from the ceiling. "But it isn't the same as being someone's very own present and finding a home on Christmas morning." For a moment Henny's eyes felt all swimmy with tears, and she had to blink three times before she could see properly again.

The minutes ticked past on the big brass clock over Barnstable's front door. Shoppers rushed to and fro, their arms piled with parcels and packages. Several people looked at Sollie admiringly and agreed that he would make a fine present—if only he weren't so dusty. One boy took a liking to Jax, until his older brother said, "But he's old! Wouldn't you rather have a new clown that does tricks?"

Soon the bell on the clock above the door began to ring. It was closing time. The shoppers vanished through the front doors, and the lights were dimmed. "Another Christmas has come and gone!" said the red-haired assistant wearily. Her name was Marianne, and she was a great favorite among the toys. "Yes," said Mrs. Dithers. "But there's no time for loitering. Hurry and straighten the place up. Remember, we open for business as usual on Monday morning."

The shop assistants raced about with their feather dusters, straightening up dolls and picking up teddy bears that had fallen over. Henny, Jax, and Sollie watched from the corner. "Another Christmas has come and gone!" said Jax. "Yes," Henny swallowed, hardly able to believe it was true.

"Oh, do try to cheer up," whispered Marianne, bending over her. "I hate to see you toys looking so miserable. Someone will give you a home yet. You'll see!"

Henny gave Marianne a grateful look. She would have said "thank you" or smiled if she could. But, of course, dolls cannot talk or smile in the presence of people—at least, not in the presence of grown-up people. Suddenly, Mrs. Dithers's face appeared, peering over Marianne's shoulder.

"What do you think you're do-ing?" The manager's eyes narrowed, and her mouth pursed in a thin line. "N-nothing, ma'am!" Marianne stammered. "Just dusting off these toys here . . ."

"A waste of time," Mrs. Dithers interrupted. "You should be seeing to the new toys, not these old things!"

Mrs. Dithers picked up Jax so roughly his cloth arms and legs flopped every which way. "Look at this sad excuse for a clown!" she declared. "He's been in the shop a year at least. And this nurse doll," Mrs. Dithers jabbed a bony finger at Henny, "Why, her uni-form isn't even white anymore! As for this lion, his mane is more gray than gold. I don't know why old Mr. Barnstable has kept these toys in the shop so long. I've told him he can't expect me to sell out-of-date merchandise. Look at them. They're completely shopworn."

Mrs. Dithers turned to Marianne. "Go at once and fetch a sack, and we'll toss them out in the rubbish."

"But, ma'am—"

"What?" Mrs. Dithers snapped.

Marianne's shoulders slumped. "Nothing."

Henny's chin began to wobble. She didn't dare look at Jax or Sollie.

Shopworn! This was the very worst thing that could ever happen to a toy, and on Christmas Eve, too. "They'll toss us out, and we'll lie forever on a rubbish heap some-where," Henny thought, "or we'll be made into rags. We'll never—" she could hardly bear to think it, "find real homes. I'll never belong to a child of my own!" Henny closed her brown glass eyes tightly.

Henny felt hands gently lift her up and place her in a big cloth sack. When she opened her eyes again, it was utterly dark. And she was being carried rapidly. "Jax! Sollie! Where are you?" she called. Although Henny was badly frightened, she managed to sound calm, for she was not a nurse doll for nothing.

"Don't worry," Jax said. His voice was reassuringly close.

"We're both right here with you," said Sollie.

Henny closed her eyes again. "I'm glad," she whispered.

"Silent night, holy night. All is calm. All is bright," Sollie sang softly beside her. Henny had never heard the song before, but thought it sounded very beautiful. "What is that song, Sollie?" she asked. "It's called 'Silent Night,'" the lion replied. "It's a Christmas song. You see, I heard a clock strike twelve just now, which means it is already Christmas."

"Oh," Henny said.

The bag stopped moving. Henny felt a bump as they were set down on a hard surface. She thought they must be in the alley, waiting with the other bags of trash to be picked up by the garbage truck. She tried to think of something cheerful to say to the other toys, but she was too afraid. She heard a bell ring, and then footsteps getting closer, and a door opening. "Marianne!" a woman cried. "There you are! I almost thought you weren't coming." They weren't in the alley after all. Marianne must have rescued them!

"Sorry," Henny heard Marianne say. "I couldn't get away earlier. But wait until you see what I've brought!"

The top of the bag opened. Henny looked up and saw the face of a strange woman smiling down at her. She was an older woman with raisin-dark eyes and round cheeks. "Oh, my!" the strange woman clapped her hands. "How ever did you get hold of such wonderful toys?"

Marianne laughed. "You'll never guess. Mrs. Dithers told me to throw them out. I couldn't believe my luck."

"Well," said the other woman. "We better hurry and get them under the tree."

Henny was lifted up into bright light. Next she was set into another box, full of soft tissue paper. Before she could have a look around to find Sollie and Jax, though, a lid was put on the box, and all went dark again. Then Henny heard a great flurry of paper rustling, and Marianne's muffled voice. "There now! Isn't that a pretty package?"

The next thing Henny knew she was flying through the air again. Soon she was set down with a thud. After that everything was very quiet. Henny was quite alone now, but she wasn't frightened. She hummed the song Sollie had sung to her. "Silent night, holy night . . ." But before she could finish it, her eyes closed and she fell fast asleep.

"Shhhhrp! Rrriiiip!" Henny woke with a start. The lid of the box flew off. Bright light was streaming in, and a face was bending over her. It was the face of a little girl with a wide mouth and shining brown eyes and hair that needed a good brushing. A girl just the right age for a doll like Henny.

"Ohhhh!" the little girl breathed. "Look! A nurse doll! Just what I've always wanted!" She picked Henny up and hugged her close. "I know you," she whispered. "You are Henny, and I am Frances, and we shall be friends for always!" Then Frances held Henny up high. "Now you must look around at your new home."

Safe in the child's arms, Nurse Henny gazed around. She was in a large room. In the middle stood a tall tree covered with brightly colored glass balls. Boys and girls were gathered around it. Henny spotted Jax being swung through the air by a girl the same age as Frances, and Sollie being hugged tightly by a boy a year or so younger. Each of the children in the room had a special toy of his or her own. Henny looked above the door of the big room and saw a string of gold paper letters that spelled, "Merry Christmas to the Children of Green Gables Orphanage!"

Later Henny learned that to many people the orphanage was a sad place, and orphanage a sad word. Yet to her it was always one of the happiest words she knew—along with Christmas—for it was there on Christmas morning that she became a child's own toy and at last found her true home.

THE WILD
SLEIGH RIDE

$\mathcal{I}$N SANTA'S WORKSHOP at the North Pole there once worked a young elf. His name was Quigley Q. Quiggleleaf, but everyone called him Quick. This was because he wanted to do everything quickly. There were so many exciting things going on at the North Pole that Quick felt he could not let a single thing escape his attention and he wanted to do everything. Sometimes he said that he one day wanted to be chief toymaker, while other times he said he wanted to grow up and be Santa's reindeer trainer. From his first day at Santa's workshop, Quick wanted to make his own toys—before he'd even had his first lesson! He also wanted to wrap his own parcels, tie his own ribbons, and design his own Christmas cards. Whenever anyone tried to show Quick how to do anything, he only said (quickly): "That's all right! I can do it by myself."

Well, perhaps. But nothing Quick did came out right. His parcels were lumpy. His ribbons were crooked. And every toy he made had something wrong with it. His teddy bears had ears like elephants, and his elephants had trunks so short they couldn't trumpet. Sometimes he even made creatures no one had ever seen before: birds with cat faces, and cats with wings!

"Oh, Quick," sighed old Hamlin, the master toy-maker elf, one day. "It's not that you don't have talent, and you certainly work hard, but you do everything too quickly. You don't listen or do as you're told. Slow down. You don't have to do everything right away. Look at me. I've been here for years, and there are still things I don't know how to do."

"Such as?" Quick said, for Hamlin seemed to know everything.

"Well, hmm, let's see . . ." said the old elf, "I don't know how to drive Santa's sleigh."

Hamlin saw at once that he had said the wrong thing, for a gleam jumped into Quick's eye. "You don't?" the young elf said. "But what fun it would be to drive Santa's sleigh on Christmas Eve! Just imagine—"

"No," Hamlin shouted. "Don't. Don't even think about it. No one drives Santa's sleigh but Santa himself. That's exactly what we've have been trying to tell you, Quick. You have to learn to walk before you can fly. Do you understand?"

"I suppose," said Quick, but the gleam in his eye didn't fade a bit.

The other elves rolled their eyes. "Now you've done it," they told Hamlin. "That young upstart thinks he can drive Santa's sleigh. He's bound to get himself into trouble!"

"No, he won't," Hamlin replied. "It's just a passing fancy. Quick will forget all about it by suppertime."

But he didn't. On the contrary, that evening when the elves had gathered in the dining hall with Santa for supper, Quick suddenly piped up from the end of the table. "Santa, this year could I—could I, please, please drive your sleigh?"

Hamlin groaned. The other elves gasped and stared, aghast. But Santa only chuckled. "So," he said, peering at Quick from behind his reading spectacles. "You want to drive my sleigh, do you? I understand. Nothing is so wonderful as driving that sleigh pulled by reindeer on Christmas Eve. But I can't let you, Quick. Driving my sleigh isn't as easy as it looks, and we wouldn't want anything to go wrong with Christmas, would we? No, you have your job, and I have mine. If I were you, I'd practice yours a bit more before you take on mine. Don't try to grow out of your boots too quickly, Quick, or you just might grow too big for them!"

The other elves laughed. Quick blushed. He felt like crying, for he knew Santa was scolding him, even though he was being nice about it.

"I'll tell you what, Quick," Santa said then. "I can't let you drive my sleigh, but I will take you along for the ride—one of these years."

The next day was Christmas Eve. Elves bustled about, putting the finishing touches on toys and games. There was so much to do, no one dared stop for a minute, but they laughed and sang as they worked. Christmas Eve is the busiest day of the year in the North Pole, but it is the happiest as well. Indeed, the only person who was not happy was Quick.

"What a fool I've been," he sighed. "How could I think Santa would let me drive his sleigh? The other elves are probably still laughing at me. Even Hamlin, who's my friend."

Just then Quick glanced out the window and spotted Santa's sleigh, sitting there all by itself, ready to go. It was hung with silver bells, and piled sky high with presents. "If only I could drive it," Quick muttered to himself. "The others wouldn't dare laugh at me then."

Suddenly, Quick remembered what Santa said the night before. "Santa said I could ride with him. . . . He said later, but I want to do it right now, this very Christmas! Why should I wait?"

Quick slipped out the workroom door and climbed into a sack of toys on the back of the sleigh. A moment later, he heard the crunch-crunch of footsteps in the snow. It was Santa, coming to start his Christmas ride. Mrs. Claus and the other elves were behind him. "Goodbye! Goodbye!" Mrs. Claus and the elves called out joyfully.

The next thing Quick knew, reindeer bells

were jingling, and the sleigh was rising high into the air. Whoosh! How fast the reindeer galloped! Quick peeked from the bag. They were way up in the night sky now, high enough to bump noses with the stars.

The reindeer swooped down, and the sleigh abruptly came to a stop. They had landed on their first roof. Down the chimney Santa went. Quick scrambled out of the toy sack (which had grown quite uncomfortable), then he caught his breath. There were lights twinkling everywhere—red, green, white, blue. Colored lights. Christmas lights!

"Oh, my," Quick whispered. "Santa was right. This is wonderful. Even more wonderful than I imagined!"

One of the reindeer—Dancer—nuzzled him on the shoulder. "Hello, there," Quick laughed. Then, before he could help himself, he thought, "As wonderful as this is, it would be more wonderful still if I could drive Santa's sleigh—just for a minute!" Quick slipped into Santa's seat (which was much too big for him), lifted the reins, and whispered, "Giddyap!"

Quick only meant to go a short distance. But the reindeer didn't know that. Up and up they leaped, over the rooftops and into the clouds! "Help!" Quick shouted. "Stop! Stop!" But the reindeer were used to obeying Santa's commands, and Quick's small voice and small tugs on the reins had no effect. On they sped, faster and faster.

Quick pulled the reins left, then right. That only made matters worse. Dasher and Dancer bolted one way, while Prancer and Vixen swung toward the other. The sleigh careened from side to side, twisting dangerously. Then—and this was so terrible Quick could hardly believe it—the sleigh flipped right over! Down the sacks of presents fell, bouncing and banging as they hit the ground. As for Quick, he went tumbling headfirst into a tall snowbank, with the sleigh on top of him. The reindeer could not pull the capsized sleigh, and they finally came to a stop, snorting and stamping.

"Oh, my goodness gracious!" Quick heard an old lady cry.

"Is that Santa's sleigh?" said a child beside her.

"It sure looks like it," said a man's voice.

58

Quick sputtered snow from his mouth and raised his head up. The bank he had landed in was in the center of a park. A group of Christmas carolers was staring at him, their mouths open wide but no songs coming forth.

"Oh, no!" Quick thought as he scrambled out from under the sleigh. "Now I've done it! I've crashed Santa's sleigh! The children's Christmas presents are scattered who-knows-where! I've ruined Christmas! Santa said I would, and I didn't listen. How could I have been such an idiot?" He hung his head. A fat tear formed in his eye and threatened to roll down to the tip of his nose. Yet before it could get there, Quick heard a high, sharp whistle. He felt a tug and another tug. He looked up.

"Well, for heaven's sake," the old lady cried. "Look!"

Quick looked. The sleigh was pulling itself out of the snowbank. "Hurry up! All aboard!" a far-away jolly voice called. Quick didn't wait for a second invitation. He scrambled back onto the sleigh, and the presents followed after him. Pop, pop, pop! Thunk, thunk, thunk! They jumped back into their sacks, just as if someone had thrown them there.

With a twisting and a rocking, the sleigh rose up from the snowbank and the reindeer quickly pulled it into the clouds. Soon they were galloping across the sky again. The next thing Quick knew, they had landed back on the very same rooftop where Quick had started his wild ride.

Santa was standing by the chimney waiting for them. He had never looked so big and bright and jolly. Quick hung his head. "Oh, Santa," he whispered. "I am so sorry. Can

you forgive me? Why, I almost—" he could barely bring himself to say the words, "ruined Christmas!"

"Ruined Christmas?" Santa shook with laughter. "Oh, Quick, it would take more than crashing my sleigh to ruin Christmas. Even if my sleigh and I didn't ride at all, there would still be Christmas. Look around you, Quick. Christmas is more than a sleigh and more than presents, and more than me. It is a feeling of joy spreading over the whole wide world."

Quick gazed at the clear night sky, at the snowy rooftops, at the lights shining all around. He thought of the elves back at the North Pole, and knew they were celebrating with food, songs, and games. He remembered the special feeling of those Christmas Eves spent surrounded by people who cared for him, and suddenly, he saw what Santa meant. He knew that Christmas was much more than toys. "Still," he said shyly. "I almost did wreck your sleigh!"

"Yes, so you did." Santa chuckled. "It was a bit harder to drive than you expected, eh? Now I suggest you let me take the reins. We have a lot of distance to cover before morning!"

"You mean—" Quick could hardly believe his ears, "you're going to take me with you?"

"Well, I can't leave you here," Santa replied. "Besides, I did say I'd take you along. I didn't mean this year, but here you are. But mind you don't try your hand at any more driving tonight!"

"Oh, no, sir," said Quick. "I won't!" And so the young elf climbed in beside Santa. The sleigh bells started to jingle as they rushed along.

The air felt cold on his face, and the stars shone ever so brightly, and the sky looked ever so vast. Beside Santa, Quick felt safe and warm. Up and down they went, and in and out of all the quiet houses. Quick helped Santa bring presents down chimneys and place them around trees and in stockings. He knew that in each house they visited lived a family as special as his own, who would wake up and celebrate the joyful holiday. He felt the spirit of Christmas spreading from house to house, a wonderful feeling connecting everyone in the whole wide world.

Even though Santa never really did scold him, Quick had learned his lesson. From that day on he was a changed elf. He listened to the older elves and learned what they had to teach, yet he never lost his independent streak. And while in time Quick did learn to make teddy bears with proper-sized ears, every so often he made a creature no one had ever seen before: an elephant with wings or a fish with feet. And he always told the younger elves to keep their dreams alive. "You never know," he said, "they might come true. Why, if you're very very lucky, you might even get to ride in Santa's sleigh!"

THE CHRISTMAS TREE

FAR TO THE NORTH, there once was a certain great forest. In that forest grew every kind of evergreen tree imaginable—blue-needled spruce, fragrant cedar, plump Scotch fir, and lodgepole pines so tall their tops almost touched the clouds.

It was a wonderful forest. All sorts of birds nested high in the tree tops. Squirrels, chipmunks, and possums made their homes in the branches. Foxes, raccoons, and rabbits dug their burrows beneath the great trunks, and herds of shy deer and elk roamed among the trees.

The great forest provided food and shelter for all these wild creatures. The tall pines gave cool shade in the summer and warm hiding places in the winter. The forest was a good place to live. In fact, it was perfect—except for one thing.

Every winter, when the forest floor lay buried under a soft blanket of snow, woodsmen came to chop down fir trees and cart them away. At first, these woodsmen only chopped down a few trees at a time. But as the years passed, and the woodsmen cut down more and more trees, the creatures of the forest grew more and more anxious.

"What can they want the trees for?" chattered the squirrels as they scurried from branch to branch, gathering nuts.

"And why do they want so many?" demanded the fox crossly, for just that year the

63

large cedar under which the fox and his family had always lived had been abruptly chopped down.

"We know," the rabbits whispered, timidly poking their heads out of their holes. Keeping an eye on the fox (whom they didn't quite trust) they explained: "We saw the trees in the vegetable market at the edge of town, where we go to steal carrots and lettuce. They were lined up all in a row, and people were buying them and taking them home."

"But what for?" huffed the possums. "People don't eat trees. And they can't use the trees for fires, because the wood is still green. So what on earth can they be doing with the trees? And why do they only buy them in wintertime?"

"I know the answer," replied Owl, who was old and wise and had traveled to more places than any of the other forest creatures. "People buy the trees because of Christmas."

"It's true!" interrupted the sparrows, for they wished to show that Owl was not the only one who had been around. "At Christmastime people bring trees into their houses and hang things on them. Bright, beautiful things, like red and green balls, and colored ropes and silver stars and—"

"Then they throw them away," said the raccoons, eager to show that they, too, were well-traveled. "We've seen them in the garbage when we go looking for a late night snack."

"But why?" asked the deer.

"Yes, why?" chimed in the elk. "What does it mean? What is this thing called Christmas?"

Everyone looked at Owl. But for once he didn't have a ready answer. "Hmmmm," he said, furrowing his brow. "Well, that's difficult to say. I know that people give each other presents at Christmastime . . ."

"And they cook lots of delicious food, too," broke in the raccoons, who liked to steal people food whenever they could.

"But as to why," Owl went on, "I don't quite know. But whatever Christmas is, it must be very special, for people always look happy at Christmas. And I've heard them singing very beautiful songs then, too."

For a moment, Owl's eyes became round and dreamy, as if he were listening to some faint, exquisite melody. Then he ruffled his feathers and continued briskly, "But that doesn't help us with our problem, which is how can we get people to stop chopping down our trees at Christmastime? Our trees. Any suggestions?"

Owl stared at each of the creatures of the forest in turn. But no one said a word. At last, a very young squirrel cleared his throat. "Umm . . ." he said.

Owl fixed his great, round eyes on the squirrel. "Yes?"

"Ummmm . . ." said the young squirrel again, for being stared at by Owl was a most intimidating experience.

"Don't just keep 'ummming,'" hooted Owl. "If you have something to say, then out with it!"

"It's what you said about presents," squeaked the nervous squirrel. "Maybe if we give the people of the town a Christmas present . . . what I mean to say is, if we decorate a tree for them right here in the forest, perhaps they won't take so many of our trees. Perhaps they'll come and see the trees here instead."

"Interesting," said the fox.

"Not a bad idea," cried the rabbits.

"Not a bad idea at all," said the deer.

"Almost a good idea," snuffled the porcupines.

"Almost a very good idea," agreed the possums.

"Yes," said Owl, cocking his head to one side, "it just might work." He furrowed his brow again and thought for a long time. At last, he said, "Since the blue spruce where I make my nest is the tallest tree in the forest, I propose that it be the tree we decorate for Christmas. And since Christmas is only one month away, and we must have our tree decorated before the woodcutters come, I propose that we begin at once!"

"Hear! Hear!" cried all the animals at once.

And so, under Owl's supervision, the work began. The sparrows flew to town and found spools of red and green thread with which to string the decorations. The squirrels gathered nuts and polished them with their little paws until they shone silver and gold. The raccoons picked red berries and pine cones and strung them into long, loopy chains. Meanwhile the cardinals and blue jays and other brightly colored birds found all the feathers they had lost and, using their nest-building skills, wove them into ornaments with their agile beaks. The deer and elk helped, too, fetching branches of holly from the forest meadows.

One by one, the animals hung these decorations on the towering blue spruce. At last, the tree was ready. The animals gathered together to admire their handiwork. Their tree had no glass balls or lights like those on other Christmas trees, yet it was no less beautiful without them. From bottom to top, the great spruce glimmered with bright berries, tufts of feathers, colorful dried leaves and flowers, and gold and silver nuts. At the very tip top was a snow-white star made from wild swan feathers, and around the bottom Owl (who prided himself on being able to read and write) had carefully arranged holly branches to spell out the words: Merry Christmas!

The animals had never seen anything like it. As they stared at their tree, a happy, joyous feeling stole over their hearts. They longed to dance across the snow and sing loud and long. They had never felt this way before, and they asked Owl, "What is this strange feeling?"

"I'm not sure," Owl replied. "But I think it is what people call the 'Christmas Spirit.'"

The next day the woodcutters came marching into the forest as they did every year. Just as they were about to chop down the first tree, one of them spotted the great spruce.

"Good heavens!" he cried. "It looks like a Christmas tree!"

"So it does," cried a second woodcutter.

"And look what it says beneath it!" cried a third.

"Merry Christmas!" read a fourth.

"It's a miracle!" they all cried at once. Without chopping down a single tree, the woodcutters ran back to town to tell people of the marvelous Christmas tree in the forest.

Soon the townspeople, young and old, came to see the wonderful Christmas tree. "How lovely," they declared when they saw it. "What unusual and exquisite decorations! Who in the world could have made them?" And they gazed around curiously, for most of them had never been so deep in the forest before. "How peaceful and beautiful it is here," they sighed. "How tall and green the trees are! And how nice the air smells, of fresh snow and pine."

As they stood there quietly, looking around and taking deep breaths of the crisp air, birds flew about and twittered and chirped. Squirrels began to chatter and dart among the tree branches. The townspeople realized that the trees they cut down every year were home to many forest creatures. If they kept taking so many, they would eventually

destroy the forest. So the townspeople decided that each year they would come into the forest and pick one tree to be the town's Christmas tree, and they would decorate it where it stood. And from then on, that is exactly what they did.

Every Christmas thereafter, the animals of the forest peered out of their holes and hiding places and the birds peeked down from their nests to watch the townspeople decorate their Christmas tree. They listened quietly as the people sang their beautiful Christmas carols. And in this way the creatures of the forest learned about Christmas, and the people of the town learned about the forest. Although the townspeople grew to truly know and love the forest, they never did learn who had decorated the great blue spruce, or how the words "Merry Christmas" came to be spelled out on the ground beneath it.

THE TEDDY BEAR
CHRISTMAS

*L*OUISA FLOPPED DOWN on her bed and looked out her window at the snow whirling down from a gray sky. "Only two more days to Christmas," she whispered excitedly to herself. Downstairs in the kitchen her mother and father were baking cinnamon star cookies to hang on the tree. The whole house smelled as good as a bakery.

Louisa glanced at the row of teddy bears placed against her pillows and frowned. "Minnie! What are you doing over there next to Koala?" She picked up a plump brown teddy bear with a green ribbon round its neck. "I was sure I put you here between Panda and Gus." She nudged a large black teddy bear that wore a mischievous expression. "And where is Benjamin? I know I set him here this morning."

Louisa poked her head under the bed. "Oh, there you are, Benjamin." She scooped up a yellow bear in a blue waistcoat. "That's the second time you've disappeared this week."

"Talking to your bears again?"

Louisa looked up at her older sister, Molly, who had come into the room. "N-no," Louisa stuttered. She knew Molly thought talking to teddy bears was for babies.

71

"Did you take the scissors out of my sewing kit?" Molly asked. "They're missing again."

"No."

"Well, the last two times they disappeared I found them under your bed."

Louisa squinted up at her older sister. "So what? But I have something to ask you. Have you been playing with my teddy bears when I'm not around?"

"Why would I want to play with your stupid teddy bears? Anyhow, Mom said to tell you to come downstairs and have some cookies while they're still warm."

"Okay. I'll be there in a minute."

Louisa listened to Molly's footsteps go down the stairs. When she couldn't hear them anymore, she looked over at her teddy bears again. "If Molly hasn't been moving you around, then who has?" she wondered aloud. Was it her imagination or did her teddy bears seem to look slightly ashamed of themselves?

Just then Louisa's hand caught on something sharp hidden in a fold in the bedspread. "Ouch!" She tugged at the bedspread. Something bright tumbled out. Molly's scissors! A piece of red wool was caught between the blades.

"Louisa!" her mother called up from the kitchen.

"Coming!"

Louisa grabbed the scissors and ran downstairs. "Hey, Molly, guess what? I found your scissors."

"Great. Where were they?"

"They were, uh, lying on my bed."

Molly frowned. "Why didn't you tell me that before?"

"I didn't know."

"I bet you did."

"I didn't!"

"Girls!" said their mother. "What's all this about?"

"She keeps taking my scissors."

"I do not!"

"Then why do they keep ending up in your room?" Molly said.

"That's a good question," said their father. He eyed Louisa over his glasses. "Are you sure you haven't been borrowing your sister's scissors?"

Louisa's cheeks felt warm. "No! I mean, yes, I'm sure."

"Then how did they get in your room?" Molly demanded.

"I don't know," Louisa said softly. "Maybe my teddy bears brought them there." She didn't mean for Molly to hear, but Molly did. "I don't believe you, Louisa," Molly said. "You keep taking my scissors, and then you blame it on your dumb teddy bears."

"My teddy bears are not dumb, and I didn't take your stupid scissors!"

"Girls, that's enough!" their mother said. "Molly, can't you be nicer to your little sister? And Louisa, you're old enough not to tell fibs when you do something wrong."

"But—" Louisa looked at her mother. Her mother seemed mad. "I'm not telling fibs," she mumbled. She took a handful of cookies and put them in her pocket. "Can I go to my room now?"

As Louisa climbed the stairs she heard her father say, "Try not to be so hard on her, Molly. She's a lot younger than you. She can't help having an over-active imagination."

Louisa bit her lip. She wasn't imagining that her teddy bears had been moved around when she wasn't looking. And who had taken Molly's scissors? Could it possibly be her bears?

Louisa took a cookie from her pocket and nibbled at it thoughtfully. Then she sighed. "I know you guys didn't mean to get me in trouble," she whispered to her teddy bears, "And I'm not mad at you. But I wish you could tell me if something is going on." For a moment Louisa had the impression that Benjamin Bear was about to say something, but of course he didn't.

The next morning was the day before Christmas. Louisa woke up early and ran downstairs to the kitchen. Her mother was already dressed. She was standing by the stove with a funny look on her face. "Louisa," she said slowly, "you didn't get up late last night and bake cookies, did you?"

"Bake cookies?"

"Yes," her mother replied. "I had a whole roll of cookie dough in the refrigerator. Now it's half gone. And there are crumbs all over the kitchen! I thought maybe you decided you didn't get enough cookies last night and . . ."

Louisa swallowed. "No, Mom. I wouldn't do that."

"Well if you didn't, who did?"

"Maybe Molly did."

Her mother shook her head. "Molly swears she had nothing to do with it. Are you sure you didn't—"

"I said no, didn't I?"

"Yes, you did." Her mother still looked doubtful. "Well, how about some breakfast. Do you want French toast or pancakes?"

"Pancakes, please."

After breakfast Louisa ran up to her room to look at her teddy bears again. Where had she put them last night? Why did she have a feeling they weren't where she'd left them? Louisa picked up Gus, who was lying at the foot of the bed. Suddenly, she noticed there was something on his face. She peered closer. "Cookie crumbs," she gasped.

"Oh, Gus," she said. "I'm disappointed in you. And in all of you," she added, with a stern glance at the others. "Why do you keep making trouble for me? And right before Christmas, too." She waited for a reply, but none of her teddy bears said a word.

That night, since it was Christmas Eve, Louisa's father made a big fire. The family sat in front of it singing Christmas carols, eating popcorn, and telling stories of past Christmases. But Louisa kept thinking about her bears. She had a nervous, jumpy feeling

inside. What would they do next?

At last the fire died down. "Time for bed," Louisa's mother announced.

"Remember, we have to give Santa time to climb down the chimney," said her father.

Louisa followed Molly up the stairs. Between waiting for Christmas morning and worrying about her mischievous teddy bears, she didn't see how she'd ever get to sleep. But she dozed off almost as soon as her head hit the pillow.

When she opened her eyes again, the moon was shining through her window—it wasn't

74

Christmas quite yet. Louisa groaned and started to roll over. Just then she heard a little silvery voice nearby whisper, "Gus! Don't eat any more of those cookies! We shouldn't have even taken that cookie dough in the first place. I knew they would notice, and we got Louisa in trouble again!"

"I said I was sorry," said a second, deeper voice. "But I couldn't resist. You know how I like cookies, and cinnamon stars are my absolute favorites."

"Oh, Gus," cried the first voice. "That's no excuse!"

Gus? Louisa inched up in the bed, noticing as she did so that her teddy bears were no longer beside her. She peeked across the room and caught her breath. Her teddy bears were sitting in a circle on the floor. All of them except Minnie. She was standing up, shaking her paw at Gus, who was hanging his head.

"Now, Minnie, getting upset won't make it better," piped up a third voice. It was a nice, calm voice, and it belonged to Benjamin Bear.

Louisa smiled, for Benjamin sounded exactly like she always thought he would. "You're right," she declared. Instantly, she clapped her hand over her mouth, for she hadn't meant to let them know she was watching. But it was too late—Benjamin, Minnie, Gus, Koala, and Panda all turned toward her.

"Oh, no!" wailed Minnie, wringing her paws together. "You've caught us!" She said this as if being caught were the worst calamity imaginable. The other bears looked as if they agreed.

"Don't worry," said Louisa. "I won't tell."

"That's not it," explained Benjamin. "We know you won't tell. It's just that no toy is ever supposed to get caught. It's one of the first rules of being a toy. Along with never getting your child into trouble . . ."

"Which we've also managed to do lately," put in Panda gloomily. "First with the scissors and then the cookies."

"Yes," sighed Gus, hanging his head even lower. "I'm afraid we've been foolish bears."

The teddy bears looked so dismayed that Louisa wanted to comfort them. "Please don't be upset," she pleaded. She climbed down from her bed to sit beside them. "The truth is I'm glad you've been so foolish. You see, I always thought you were alive, but I

never knew for certain and now . . ." Louisa looked at her bears and grinned. The bears grinned back.

"But," she went on after a moment, "tell me one thing. Why have you bears been so naughty lately? You were always so quiet and well-behaved before."

"Because of Christmas," said Benjamin Bear, as if that would explain everything.

"Yes," added Minnie. "We teddy bears have never had a Christmas of our own before. But after watching you and your family celebrate Christmas year after year we decided that this year we'd have a Christmas of our own."

"With a teddy bear Christmas tree," said Panda.

"And a teddy bear Christmas dinner," said Gus.

"And teddy bear Christmas presents," Minnie said. She glanced at Louisa shyly. "We even made you a Christmas present. That's why we needed the scissors."

"Minnie!" scolded Panda. "You shouldn't have told her! It's supposed to be a surprise."

"But it is Christmas," said Koala stoutly. "It's one minute past midnight."

"Hooray!" cried the other bears. "Let's give her her present now!" Minnie and Benjamin waddled over to the bookshelf. From behind a thick volume of fairy tales, they pulled out a small package, which was wrapped in brown paper and tied with a red ribbon.

"Go on, open it," said Benjamin.

Inside was the neatest, prettiest pair of mittens Louisa had ever seen. They were made of red and green wool, and across each wrist marched a row of teddy bears. Not just any teddy bears, but her teddy bears. Tiny little Minnies and Benjamins and Guses and Koalas and Pandas danced across each mitten, which fit Louisa's hands perfectly.

"Do you like them?" asked Benjamin Bear anxiously.

"Oh, yes," Louisa replied.

"I fetched the wool," said Gus in his deep gruff voice.

"And I made up the design," announced Koala.

"I helped," Panda reminded him.

"And Minnie knitted them," Benjamin Bear said proudly.

"They're beautiful," said Louisa. "The most beautiful mittens I ever saw."

"Merry Christmas," said the teddy bears.

"Merry Christmas," Louisa said. Then the teddy bears showed her their tiny Christmas tree (made from branches Louisa's dad had trimmed from the family's tree downstairs) and their presents, and the sweets and cookies they had set aside for their first ever teddy bear Christmas dinner. Louisa hugged them all and fell fast asleep and didn't wake up again until Christmas morning.

"What great mittens," said Molly, as she and Louisa sat under the Christmas tree opening their presents.

"Yes, they're lovely," their mother said. "Where in the world did you get them, Louisa?"

"Uh, from some secret admirers, I guess," Louisa replied.

Just then there was a bump

from upstairs, a dull bump as if something had fallen off a chair. It was followed by a faint pitter-patter like little paws padding across the floor.

"Did you hear that?" said Louisa's father. "I should go upstairs and check. It sounds like mice."

"Oh, no, don't," said Louisa quickly. "It's probably nothing," for she was almost sure that it was her teddy bears, celebrating their very first teddy bear Christmas.

THE REAL
SANTA CLAUS

*J*ONATHAN COULD HARDLY believe his eyes. Santa Claus was standing across the street in front of Griswold's Department Store. He tugged at his older brother Will's sleeve. "Look!" he shouted. "There's Santa. Can we go see him. Can I go give him my letter? Pleeease?"

Jonathan felt the letter in his pocket. It had taken him most of the night to write it. "To Mr. S. Claus," it said on the envelope. "The North Pole, Planet Earth, The Universe."

"Will? Will? Can you hear me? Santa's over there! Can we please go give him my letter?"

Will didn't even turn around. *"Uh-uh."* he said.

"We can't?" Jonathan could hardly believe his ears. "But—"

"No," Will repeated. "We have too much Christmas shopping to do. Anyway, that guy isn't really Santa Claus."

"What do you mean?" asked Jonathan. "How do you know?"

Will sighed. "There is no such person as Santa Claus."

Jonathan stared at him. He couldn't believe his brother would say such a terrible thing. "You're lying!"

Will shrugged. "Have it your way. But I'm telling you, Santa Claus doesn't exist. Look, I'll prove it. Come on."

Will dragged Jonathan across the street. "Ho! Ho! Ho!" the Santa Claus said as they walked up. "Merry Christmas! Come on in and enjoy Griswold's Holiday Extravaganza! Ho! Ho! Ho!"

"That's okay, Mr. Santa Claus," Will said. "But if you don't mind, my little brother wants to ask you a question." He nudged Jonathan. "Go on. Ask him if he's real."

Jonathan looked up at the Santa Claus. "A-a-re you the real Santa?" he stammered.

"Ho! Ho! Ho! That's a good question, kid. Am I the real Santa? Of course, I am!"

"So you live in the North Pole with Mrs. Santa and the elves," Jonathan asked eagerly, "and you have reindeer and everything?"

"Well, uh, not exactly." The Santa's cheeks turned as red as his suit. "Sorry, kid, I can't lie to you. I'm not the real Santa Claus. I'm just a regular guy doing a job." He jerked his thumb in the direction of Griswold's Department Store.

"See, the store pays me to dress up as Santa every Christmas."

"Oh," said Jonathan.

"Yeah, I'm a big fake," sighed the Santa Claus. He reached in his pocket and pulled out a candy cane. "Here, kid. Come on, don't look so down! Just because I'm not the real thing doesn't mean there isn't a real Santa someplace. . . ."

"Thanks." Jonathan turned away. He didn't want to hear any more, though he knew the fake Santa was only trying to be nice. No real Santa Claus? Jonathan fingered the letter in his pocket again. He wondered if he should even bother to mail it. He followed Will back across the street.

"Are you mad at me?" his brother asked.

"No," Jonathan said, but he was—a little. Why did

82

Will always have to be right? "Maybe the fake Santa was telling the truth," he thought, "and there is a real Santa Claus somewhere." But as Jonathan looked around the busy shopping street, he had to admit that it didn't seem likely. There were Santas everywhere, but not one of them looked real.

One Santa had a cotton-wool beard that was half-falling off his face. Another was chewing bubble gum. Somehow Jonathan couldn't imagine the real Santa Claus chewing bubble gum. Still another Santa was saying to the man next to him, "I can't wait to get out of this dumb red suit. It itches! Plus these boots are too tight. My feet are killing me!"

They were all big fakes.

Will stopped in front of a record store. "I need to go in here for a minute," he said. "Will you be okay alone out here?"

"Sure." Jonathan watched Will disappear through the swinging doors. Then he took his letter to Santa out of his pocket and slowly walked over to the big trash can by the curb.

"Hold on a minute," said a voice. Someone snatched the letter out of his hand. Jonathan whirled around. An old man was standing there. "Hey! That's my letter!" Jonathan said.

"So it is," said the old man. He had a deep, rumbly, yet friendly sounding voice. "However, I couldn't help noticing you were about to throw this letter away instead of mailing it."

"So?" said Jonathan.

"So," said the old man. "That's an awfully sad thing to do to a letter."

The old man stared at Jonathan with a worried look on his face. He had a long white beard, bright twinkling eyes, and was wider in the belly than he was anywhere else. In

83

fact, he looked a bit like Santa Claus, only Santa Claus never looked worried. Besides, instead of a red suit, the old man was wearing a dusty blue coat. And instead of shiny leather boots, he had on a worn pair of black, high-top sneakers.

"I don't see why it's such a sad thing to do to a letter," Jonathan said. "Anyhow, it's *my* letter. Can't a person throw away his own letter if he wants to?"

"I suppose," said the old man. Then he sighed. It was the loudest, saddest-sounding sigh Jonathan had ever heard. It seemed to start at the tips of his black sneakers and travel all the way up to the top of his head.

"Are you all right?"

"Fine," sniffed the old man. But he didn't sound fine.

"Come on," said Jonathan. "What's the matter?"

"Oh, it's nothing really," the old man replied. "It's just this letter of yours. I wish you wouldn't throw it away."

"Why not?" said Jonathan. "What do you care? Anyway, it's none of your business—"

"That's where you're wrong," the old man interrupted. "It *is* my business. Most definitely my business. You see, this letter of yours is addressed to me!"

Jonathan's mouth fell open. "You mean you're . . ."

The old man nodded. "The one and only."

Jonathan eyed the old man's blue coat and his high-top sneakers. Could it be true? Then he remembered all the other Santa Clauses. None of them were real. Why should this Santa Claus be any different? "You're crazy," he said.

Most people would have gotten mad at being called crazy. But the old man didn't seem to mind. He only sighed again. "I was afraid you'd say that," he said. "It's worse than the measles, and it's spreading everywhere these days."

"What's spreading everywhere?" asked Jonathan nervously.

"Doubt," the old man replied. "Doubt and disbelief. It's a wonder anyone believes in me anymore."

The old man looked so sad that Jonathan felt awful, even worse than he felt when Will first told him there was no Santa Claus. He peered at the old man sideways. Of course, he probably wasn't the real Santa Claus, but he might be. "He thinks he is anyway," Jonathan thought, "and I really hurt his feelings." Jonathan took a deep breath. "Uh, I don't really think you're crazy," he said aloud.

"That's okay," said the old man.

"I mean, I do believe in you, sort of. Honest I do. My brother only just now told me you aren't real. I guess I just expected you to be wearing your red suit, you know?"

"Oh, that old outfit," said the old man. "I almost never go around dressed in that. I'm afraid that red suit of mine is awfully warm for everyday wear."

"I guess it must be," said Jonathan. "But just so you know, I believe in you and everything. . . ."

The old man beamed at him. "Glad to hear it," he said. "because I believe in you, too."

It was a strange thing to say. And if anyone else had said it, Jonathan would have been embarrassed. But somehow the old man sounded as if he truly meant it.

"Thanks," Jonathan said.

"No, thank *you,* Jonathan."

"Hey! How do you know my name?"

The old man didn't answer. Jonathan gazed up at him. All of a sudden, Jonathan was sure he was Santa Claus. "You're welcome, sir," said Jonathan. He shook Santa Claus's hand. "And about that letter I wrote you, I know I asked for lots of toys, but you don't have to get them all for me."

"I'll use my judgment," Santa Claus said.

"I just don't want you to think I'm spoiled or anything."

"I won't."

"The truth is, you don't have to get me anything if you don't want to. Although I would like, um . . . "

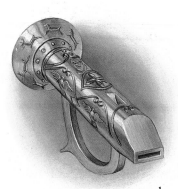

"Yes? What would you like?"

"I'd like to see your reindeer," Jonathan faltered, "if it's not too much trouble. If I could see your reindeer, I wouldn't even want any presents. Or maybe just one tiny little present."

"I see," said Santa. He opened his mouth and laughed a real Santa laugh. "Well, Jonathan," he said, "it's not every day I let someone see my reindeer. They're very shy creatures, you know. But then again, it's not every day I get someone to believe in me without any proof. And so—" Santa pulled a tiny silver whistle from his pocket "—just blow on this and I, my sleigh, and my reindeer will appear before you, wherever you are."

"Are you serious?"

"Perfectly serious," Santa Claus said. "But if I were you, I'd use that whistle soon. I'm getting busier by the day, and on Christmas Eve it will become just an ordinary silver whistle again."

"But if I blow on it now, I'll see your sleigh and all the reindeer, too?"

"That's what I said isn't it?" Santa Claus smiled.

"But won't all these people scare the reindeer?" Jonathan demanded. "Won't they all rush at you and . . ."

"I'll bet only one or two of them will even see me," replied Santa Claus softly.

"You mean—"

"I mean, you can't see what you don't believe in. Go on, give it a whistle." Santa's voice trailed off in a funny way. Jonathan looked up. Santa was gone, and so was Jonathan's letter.

"Wow," Jonathan said. Just as Will came out of the record store, Jonathan lifted the silver whistle to his lips. He blew long and hard. The whistle made no noise he could hear. But suddenly, just in front of him, about four feet off the sidewalk, Jonathan saw a beautiful silver sleigh harnessed to eight bright-eyed reindeer. The old man was sitting in the sleigh. He was dressed in his red Santa suit now. Yet on his feet he was still wearing his high-top sneakers.

"Hi!" Jonathan waved.

"Hi!" Santa waved back. "Ho! Ho! Ho! Merry Christmas, Jonathan! Merry Christmas!"

The reindeer tossed their heads, stamped their silver hooves, and jingled all their bells. Then Santa snapped the reins, and all together they rose high above the busy street.

"Hey," said Will, shaking Jonathan by the shoulder. "Wake up. You're daydreaming. Want to go across the street and say hi to Santa Claus?" Will pointed to a Santa Claus standing on the corner, ringing a big brass bell.

"Uh-uh," Jonathan said. "He's not the real Santa Claus."

"So you're finally wising up," said Will.

For a moment Jonathan almost told his brother about how he'd met the real Santa Claus and seen his sleigh and reindeer, but he knew Will would only laugh at him. As Santa Claus had said, "You can't see what you don't believe in."

"Not exactly," Jonathan murmured.

"What do you mean not exactly?" asked Will.

Jonathan closed his fingers around the tiny silver whistle. "I mean *not exactly*," he said. And he smiled.

THE AMAZING ADVENTURE
OF MARCO McSWEENEY

*I*T WAS A COLD GRAY DAY, about two weeks before Christmas, and Marco McSweeney was bored. But unlike most bored boys, Marco did not sit around moaning and groaning. Instead, he turned to his younger sister and trusted co-conspirator, Tink.

"Tink, I am bored," Marco said. "It's time to take action. I have decided to do something so amazing that kids all over the world will be talking about it for years and years!"

"Oh, Marco," Tink groaned. She knew her brother well enough to know that this something—whatever it was—would probably mean Big Trouble. "Are you sure? Don't you want to think about it some more?"

"I have thought about it," Marco replied. "In fact, I have a plan. I am going to mail myself to the North Pole for Christmas."

If she'd been sitting, Tink would have fallen out of her seat. "Marco, you can't do that!"

"Why not?"

"Because no one's ever done it before. I bet it's dangerous. And you should spend Christmas here with Mom and Dad and me!"

"I do that every year," said Marco. "But Christmas in the North Pole will be an incredible adventure. I'll need your help."

"No way." Tink shook her head.

"Pleeease?"

"Well . . . if you give me half your collection of jumbo gum balls."

"It's a deal," said Marco.

With Tink's help, Marco found a sturdy cardboard box. He punched some air holes in the top and laid his Ranger Rick sleeping bag on the bottom. He packed thirteen peanut-butter-and-jelly sandwiches, a bag of barbeque potato chips, and a deluxe-sized box of candy canes, because it was almost Christmas. He also packed a carton of apple juice, twelve cans of root beer, and a thermos of hot chocolate with mini-marshmallows.

"Now don't forget to dress warmly," Tink reminded him. "You are going to the North Pole, after all."

"I will," promised Marco. He put on four pairs of socks, three sweaters, two coats, three scarves, two mittens on each hand, and a pair of earmuffs. Then he was ready to go.

He lumbered into the box and pulled the flaps closed over his head. "All right, Tink," he shouted. "Tape me shut. Don't forget to write Santa's address in big letters on the top. And make sure you put on all those stamps I gave you."

"Don't worry," Tink said. Soon the mailman came, and Marco was on his way.

It was a long, long journey. Of course, Marco could never see where he was, but he could feel himself getting jogged, jiggled, bounced, and bumped. Mail carriers lugged him here and there. They put Marco on trucks and took him off trucks. They stuck him in the mail compartments of trains and even in the hold of a jet airplane. At last, just when Marco thought he would never get to his destination (and long after his peanut-butter-and-jelly sandwiches had run out), he heard the pilot shout, "Last stop! The North Pole!"

Marco's box was set down on something soft and cold. Marco poked his head out of the box. He was in the middle of a snowy field. A short distance away stood a cozy, rambling stone house. Candy canes hung in the windows, and a crooked chimney gave off puffs of pine-scented smoke. "Santa's house!" Marco whispered. "Boy, am I glad to be here!"

Just then Marco saw two stout little figures huffing towards him across the snow. They were dressed in bright green coats and long red hats. They had round-as-apple cheeks and bright, sparkling eyes. "Santa's elves!" Marco breathed. He quickly ducked down again before they could see him. Marco felt the box being lifted shakily into the air.

"Whew!" said one of the elves. "I've never known Mr. C. to get a letter this heavy!"

"Me either," grunted the other elf. "This letter is so heavy it might squash us both flat as bugs. Thank goodness we don't have far to go!"

Soon Marco and the box were set down with a great big thud.

"What in the name of Christmas is in that box?" said the first elf.

"Maybe we should open it and take a peek," suggested the second. Inside the box, Marco caught his breath.

"Maybe," said the first elf. "But you know how Mr. C. is about his mail. He likes to open every piece himself. He says it wouldn't be fair to the children otherwise."

"Mr. C. is right, of course," sighed the second. "Still, I'd like to know what's in this box. It's so heavy, and as we were going along I thought I heard something in there breathing."

"Breathing?" gasped the first. "Are you sure? Dear me, we'd better go tell Mr. C. at once!"

The two elves padded off with quick little steps. Marco cautiously climbed out of the box. He was in Santa's mail room! It was piled to the ceiling with letters and packages and parcels. Some were in red envelopes, some in green. Some were tied with ribbon, others with string. Marco had never seen so much mail in his life. Just the thought of opening and reading it all made his fingers and his eyes ache. "How in the world does Santa do it?" Marco wondered.

Just then the door burst open, and there stood the two elves who had carried him in.

"So there *was* someone in the box!" said the first.

"A boy, by Christmas!" said the second.

At least, that's what Marco thought he said. He didn't wait to be sure. Quick as a wink, he slipped past the elves and raced down a narrow hallway.

The hallway wound past big doors and small doors and medium-sized ones. There were so many doors Marco couldn't decide which one to go through. And as he was trying to make up his mind, Marco smelled a delicious smell. At first it smelled like fudge cooking, then like sugar cookies fresh out of the oven. Then it smelled of cinnamon and fruit, like the Christmas cakes his grandmother sometimes made. Marco's nose began to twitch. He followed the wonderful smell to a green door which was open just a crack. Marco peered inside.

He saw a large kitchen that had an enormous pot-bellied stove in one corner. At a long table, a jolly, gray-haired woman who could only be Mrs. Santa Claus was mixing cookie dough in a huge bowl. All around her little elves were busily cooking all kinds of Christmas treats. Some were whipping up batches of fudge and some were steaming Christmas puddings. Others were rolling out pie dough. Still others were pulling trays of freshly baked Christmas cookies from the depths of the warm oven. Marco's mouth began to water, for by now he was really very hungry. "If only I could have just have one cookie," he thought.

Marco stretched out his arm toward the nearest tray that was cooling on the kitchen counter. One cookie was all he meant to take, but by accident, he grabbed the entire tray instead.

"Stop! Stop! What do you think you're doing?" cried an elf wearing a tall red chef's hat.

Marco turned and dashed down the hall, holding the tray of cookies in front of him. He could hear little elf footsteps pounding behind him, and elves calling out in tiny excited voices, "Stop, thief! Stop!"

"It isn't fair!" Marco muttered between mouthfuls of cookies. "I'm not really a thief. I only stole these cookies because I was hungry!" He thought of Tink and his mother and father back home, and the Christmas cookies they always made together every year. They weren't nearly as good as these cookies, but he didn't have to steal them either. For a moment he wished he were back home, but then he reminded himself that real adventurers never get homesick.

"There he is! Stop him! Stop him!"

Marco ducked through a doorway and found himself in a large, barnlike room. Long wooden tables filled the room. Elves wearing green aprons were bent over these tables, and each elf was making a toy. Marco's heart quickened. He realized he must be in the most important place in the North Pole—Santa's secret toy workshop! Marco edged his way into the room. A large wooden cupboard stood in a corner. Marco slipped inside it and pulled the door half shut. From this hiding place, he peered out at the workshop.

It was a marvelous place. The walls were lined with brightly painted shelves, and on them was every kind of toy imaginable. There were toy soldiers, princess dolls, clowns, stuffed toy monkeys, elephants, and hippopotami. There were toy cars, boats, trains, and airplanes. There were little toy castles and fortresses and even a toy city with toy skyscrapers and toy parks and a toy zoo.

Despite how amazing Santa's workshop was, Marco felt something was wrong. At first, he couldn't put his finger on it. Then it came to him. Christmas was only a week away, yet Santa's elves were not laughing or whistling as they worked. Instead, they looked solemn and anxious. And one elf—an important-looking elf in a red apron— looked positively miserable.

This elf gazed around the room at the toys the other elves were working on and sighed. "To think I used to be good at my job," he said. "Santa's chief toy designer, and now I can't design a decent toy no matter what I do. Everything I turn my hand to comes out dull, dull, dull."

"Don't be silly, Hamlin," an elf piped up. "That's not true," another elf said to him. But Hamlin only shook his head and said, "It's nice of you to say so, but I know dull when I see it."

Marco cautiously poked his head out of the cupboard. He stared at the toy that the elf to his right was making. It was a green train. There was nothing wrong with it, but it wasn't exactly exciting. He looked at the toy in the hands of the elf to his left. It was a clown dressed in red and blue. It was a perfectly nice clown, but not very different from the toy clowns Marco had seen last year or the year before.

"The truth is, I'm all washed up," Hamlin elf declared. "It's time Santa found himself a new chief toy designer."

The elf looked so forlorn Marco couldn't help feeling sorry for him. "If only I could do something to help," Marco thought. "But if I show myself, these elves will probably just start chasing me like the others did." Then, since it was very hot and stuffy in the cupboard, Marco began to yawn. Before he knew it, he was fast asleep.

When Marco woke up it was night. The workshop was empty. Marco tiptoed out of the cupboard. Stars were shining through the windows. The toys the elves had been working on were still on the work tables. Marco looked at them. There was the toy train, and the clown, and a toy truck, and a stuffed elephant, and a fairy princess doll in a long golden dress. "There's nothing really wrong with these toys," Marco said to himself. "They just need some touching up—something to make them new and different." So he switched on a lamp, sat down at the workbench, and set to work.

Marco painted purple and orange stripes on the side of the green train and added a

zoo car, and red headlights to the front. He turned the clown into an acrobat and stood him on his head and painted moons and stars on his face. He gave the stuffed elephant the fairy princess's wings, and made the fairy princess into a pirate wearing a three-cornered newspaper hat and a patch over her eye. "That's better," Marco said. He changed the truck into a fire engine with an extra-loud siren. However, he made the mistake of trying out the siren one time too many.

"There he is, the boy who was hiding in the box!"

"There he is, the boy who stole our cookies!"

"What's he doing in our workshop?"

The two elves from Santa's mail room had burst into the workshop, followed by the baker elf in his tall red chef's hat. Next came the toy-making elves, with Santa's chief toy designer, Hamlin elf, close behind. Lastly, in came Mrs. Santa Claus, and with her was the round jolly figure of Santa Claus himself.

Marco looked at the elves. He looked at Santa and Mrs. Claus. He couldn't tell if Santa was mad or not. "Boy, I bet he is, though," Marco thought. "He probably doesn't like people sneaking into his house . . . or stealing his cookies . . . or messing up his toys." Marco hung his head and wished he could just disappear. In fact, he wished he were safely back home. But just then a voice cried out,

"But this is fabulous! Look at these! The boy's a genius!"

95

It was Hamlin elf. He was staring at the toys Marco had fixed up and grinning from ear to ear. "Look, Mr. C.! Look at what he's done to the toys!"

Santa looked, and he began to smile, too. So did Mrs. Claus and the other elves—even the elf in the chef's hat, who had called Marco a thief.

"He's saved Christmas for us!" declared Hamlin elf. "Thanks to him, we won't have to give the children dull toys."

"Indeed he has," agreed Santa. "Well done, Marco."

Before Marco could ask Santa how he knew his name, Hamlin and the other elves cried, "Hooray! Hooray for Marco!" They cheered him for such a long time that Marco began to get embarrassed. "Aw, it was nothing," he said.

"Maybe to you," Santa Claus replied. "But I'm afraid we were at our wits' end. We've been making toys for so many years that we were getting stale. You came just in the nick of time, and you are just what we need— a real child to look over our work. Since you were resourceful enough to come all the way here on your own, Marco, perhaps you'd like to stay on as our official toy consultant. You could look over our toys for us and tell us what—if anything—needs to be done to improve them."

"Do you really mean it?" Marco cried.

"Yes I do," said Santa, and his eyes twinkled. Marco grinned, then his grin faded.

"I - I'd like to help you," he stammered. "But if I do, do I have to stay here forever? The North Pole is a terrific place and everything, but I kind of miss home."

"I expect you do," Santa said. "That's the real reason we've been chasing you. You see, this letter came for me yesterday by special

96

delivery, and we've been on the lookout for you ever since." Santa handed Marco an already opened letter. Marco glanced down at it. It was in Tink's handwriting.

Marco began to read:

Dear Santa,

Do you have a boy there called Marco McSweeney? He is my brother. He mailed himself to you a week ago. I hope he has gotten there safely. If he has, could you please send him home again? Everyone here is sad without him. Mom keeps sighing and Dad keeps frowning. They won't even put up a tree or make Christmas cookies until Marco comes home. I tried to tell them he was with you, but they just said, "Then tell Santa to send him home on the double!" To tell the truth, I miss Marco, too. So please send him home for Christmas

Yours truly,
Tink McSweeney

P.S. If you do, you don't even have to give me any toys this year. Or not very many.

P.P.S. Thank you, Santa. We're counting on you!

Marco blinked. "Gee," he said. "I didn't think they'd miss me that much."

"Well, they do," said Santa. "That's why I thought I'd take my sleigh out tonight, especially for you, so that you can get home in time for Christmas."

"You mean I get to ride in your sleigh? With the reindeer and everything?" said Marco. "Yippee!"

So Santa took Marco home. Santa's reindeer pulled the sleigh high into the sky until Marco could reach out and touch the clouds. Below him, he could see the snowy fields of the North Pole. Seals and polar bears bustled to and fro, preparing for their Christmas celebrations. Than Santa pulled the reins to one side, saying, "I thought just this once we'd go the long way around."

"Yippee!" said Marco, for he guessed that this meant he was about to take a trip around the world. And he was!

Santa's sleigh soared over the North Atlantic Ocean, past Iceland and Greenland, and over Denmark, Sweden, and Norway. Peeping over the edge of the sleigh, Marco saw tiny wooden houses. In their windows he saw candles flickering and children gathered around fires, listening to long, wonderful Christmas tales.

Soon the sleigh was crossing over Russia. Huge, snow-covered pine forests stretched out beneath Marco. The reindeer, liking the smell of pine (for it reminded them of their wild homeland), tossed their heads, making their bells jingle. Below, horses pulled a sled quickly through the snowy darkness. A grandfather was driving it, and in the back seat his grandchildren, all bundled up in thick fur coats and fur hats, squealed with delight.

Marco smiled at what he'd seen. But the journey wasn't even half over. Santa drove the sleigh over Mongolia and across the north of China. Marco could see the great Yangtze River lined with boats of all shapes and sizes. Some of them were houseboats lit up with red paper lanterns. From one of them came a sound both strange and familiar. Someone was singing "Silent Night, Holy Night," but in Chinese!

"Wow," Marco whispered.

Santa turned to him. "You're not getting cold, are you?" Marco shook his head. "Or hungry?" Santa asked.

"No, sir!" Marco grinned. He had been nibbling on cookies that Mrs. Claus had given him for the ride.

"Glad to hear it!" Santa chuckled. "Now give me a cookie, Marco, my boy, and on we go!"

The two of them munched happily on gingerbread cookies as the sleigh sped just a little bit above the sharply peaked mountains of Tibet. They saw elephants sleeping under glittering temples in India, where the leaves on the palm trees were fluttering in a night breeze. It was as warm as summer now, and the air smelled of flowers. You wouldn't even know it was Christmastime, except for the colored lights hung in windows below. Marco threw his blankets into a corner of the sleigh and then took off his coat and sweater.

The sleigh traveled on across the great Sahara Desert and over Turkey and Greece. Above Italy, Santa slowed the reindeer so they could rest. As they floated in the sky, Marco leaned over the edge of the sleigh to peer at the ancient city of Rome. Its stone buildings and statues gleamed softly in the darkness, and a cool wind blew from the Alps in the north. Marco put on his warm clothes again.

When the reindeer were rested, they zoomed off quicker than ever—so fast that Marco almost fell out of his seat. But luckily Santa reined them in just in time. "Whoa,

Dancer and Prancer, Donner and Blixen!" he shouted. The reindeer jingled their bells impatiently but continued at a slower pace.

They flew across Spain and France. Marco's eyes grew wide when they sailed over the beautiful city of Paris, but he was even more excited when they crossed the English Channel and flew over London. Beneath him was the famous clock Big Ben, and it was striking midnight. "Clang! Clang! Clang!" rang the big bells. Marco could see lighted Christmas trees in the town square below. He could smell plum puddings and pies baking, but best of all, he could hear music rising from the streets below. Christmas carolers were gathered together, singing "O Little Town of Bethlehem," one of Marco's favorites.

Marco blinked and felt a funny lump in his throat. "Christmas is the greatest," he said to Santa solemnly.

Santa nodded his head. "It certainly is," he agreed.

Then the sleigh sped off over the endless glittering Atlantic Ocean. Now there was nothing to see but bright waves and sea birds and stars. Marco felt warm and drowsy, and his head began to nod down onto his chest. The next thing he knew, Santa was shaking him and saying, "Wake up, Marco, my boy. You're home."

Marco opened his eyes and saw his very own house, with a light shining in the window. He had traveled to every country in the world tonight and seen many incredible sights, but somehow this familiar one was the best of all. "Down the chimney you go!" Santa said with a grin. "And don't worry about getting hurt or dusty, for

anyone who has been to the North Pole has a share in Christmas magic. And that means you can go down chimneys without the least bit of trouble."

"Really?" said Marco doubtfully.

"Give it a try, you'll see. And Merry Christmas, Marco!" Santa and his sleigh rose up and up into the sky. Marco hesitated a moment, and then—zip!—down the chimney he slid.

"Hello!" he cried as he stumbled into the living room. "Hello, I'm home!"

His mother and father and Tink were overjoyed to see him. Indeed, it was the McSweeney family's best Christmas ever, and Santa brought everyone lots and lots of presents. As for Marco, after his great adventure he did travel to the North Pole from time to time to help Hamlin with his toy designs. Eventually he became close friends with all the elves, even the chef elf who had scared him so much on his first visit. But although Marco liked the North Pole better each time he visited, he always said that the best place to spend Christmas was in your very own house, with your very own family.

• Stories by Sheila Black •

The text of this book was set in Adobe Stempel Garamond
and the initial caps in Snell Roundhand.

Type was set by Diane Stevenson of Snap Haus Graphics in Dumont, New Jersey.
Title and introduction calligraphy are by Rosemary Morrissey-Herzberg.
This book was printed by Tien Wah Press in Singapore.

Interior illustrations by the following artists

Christmas Tree Soup • James Bernardin
Snowball, the Naughty Christmas Kitten • Robyn Officer
Ichod, the Ice Troll • Richard Bernal
The Perfect Christmas Present • Teresa Fasolino
A Christmas Angel • Ruth Sanderson
A Toy's Christmas • Robyn Officer
The Wild Sleigh Ride • Jerry Tiritilli
The Christmas Tree • John Berkey
The Teddy Bear Christmas • Ruth Sanderson
The Real Santa Claus • James J. Himsworth III
The Amazing Adventure of Marco McSweeney • Paul Selwyn